Someone to come
HOME TO

SOMEONE SERIES BOOK 2

Someone to Come HOME TO

ROBERT LEWIS

4 Horsemen
Publications, Inc.

4 Horsemen
Publications, Inc.

4 Horsemen Publications, Inc.
1497 Main St. Suite 169
Dunedin, FL 34698
4horsemenpublications.com
info@4horsemenpublications.com

Cover b y S. Wilder
Typesetting by Autumn Skye
Editor: Shirley Austin

Library of Congress Control Number: 2022941726

Paperback ISBN-13: 978-1-64450-674-5
Audiobook ISBN-13: 978-1-64450-672-1
Ebook ISBN-13: 978-1-64450-673-8

Dedication

T<small>HIS IS **DEDICATED**</small> to all the dreamers. May your dreams come true, like mine have.

Table of Contents

SUMMER OF 89ING

BILLY BASKED UNDER the warm sun in the park, surrounded by people busy carving out their own little spot to enjoy the weather. Children laughed, dogs barked, and in the distance, he could hear people enjoying the park. He tried to tune them out, focusing on the music which played in his ears, but they filtered in anyhow.

The sounds reminded him of days long past: days when things for him were more simple and carefree, before he understood men lied to get what they wanted from him, and before he knew the people who were supposed to love him unconditionally would cast him aside for their own happiness.

It was the summer after his high school graduation, back when life was all rainbows and unicorns. Billy was eighteen—a man now—or so he told people. The truth was he was still a foolish, naive boy who had no clue how the real world worked. If he had, he would have saved himself a ton of heartache and had a plan.

Of course not having a plan landed him where he was now. *If you're going to run, make sure you know what you're running toward,* Billy told himself, wishing he knew that the day everything started to change.

Billy had snuck out of the house in his cut-offs and homemade crop top. His mom was at work, while her latest loser boyfriend was loafing on the couch, the only thing he was good for. Well, it wasn't the *only* thing he was good for, if the sounds from his mother's bedroom were any indication.

Billy snuck straight into the woods behind his house, following the path he and his friends had worn into the ground over the years. The air was moist and cool under the canopy of the trees. He made his way through until he arrived at the little clearing where the huge oak tree grew.

There, he found Teddy waiting for him—lying on a blanket, shirtless and wearing the shortest running shorts. Billy took a moment to take him all in: his long, lean legs; his hard, flat stomach with just the hint of definition; and his ruby-red nipples centered perfectly on his exquisitely etched pecs.

Teddy's eyelids fluttered open, revealing his icy-blue eyes that warmed Billy's heart. Teddy's full lips curled into a crooked grin. The hard line of his jaw looked freshly shaven; Billy knew it rarely saw the glide of a razor. The only thing Teddy shaved regularly was his balls.

Teddy asked, cocky as always, "What are you looking at? Are you one of those fags?"

Billy crossed his arms over his chest. "You know I am. What are you going to do about it?"

Teddy sat up on his elbows. "You want to find out?" Billy could see Teddy's cock harden, poking out of his shorts. "Come here and I'll show you."

"Definitely." Billy tried not to laugh at their silly game as he lay down on top of Teddy, pressing his own hard cock into Teddy's. "You think you're man enough to show me?"

"Shut up and kiss me." Teddy took Billy by the back of the head and pulled him into a hungry kiss. Falling back, he took Billy in his arms, his hands exploring the familiar forbidden territory of Billy's back. "I'm going to miss this when I'm at collage."

"I guess you're going to have to convince your frigid girlfriend to finally put out," Billy teased, rutting his hips against Teddy's. "I can teach her what you like, if you want." Billy was flipped onto his back, and Teddy was glaring down at him, holding his hands down and straddling his waist. "Hey!"

"That's not funny," Teddy seethed. Billy saw the flash of anger in his eyes, anger Teddy had for himself, at their situation, at Billy. "You know if what we do gets out, it could keep me from actually having a baseball career."

"You know you'll be the MVP of the Super Bowl, then I'll point and say, 'I blew him,'" Billy needled.

Teddy groaned, his anger subsiding. "That's *foot-ball*, but you knew that, you jerk." Teddy dove into him, sucking on Billy's sensitive neck. Billy's hips thrust up automatically, pressing his hard cock against

Teddy's ass. "What do you think you're doing?" Teddy looked down at the grinning Billy.

Billy winked. "You liked it that one time. After that game when we got tipsy on that cheap wine I got."

"That was a one-time thing. My dick goes in your ass, not the other way around," Teddy growled.

Billy ground his cock against Teddy's ass again. Teddy involuntarily moaned. "Is that right? Doesn't sound like you want it to be."

"Yeah, well, you want *this* dick more." Teddy pushed Billy's hips down with his ass. "That's why you keep coming back for more." Teddy rose up and flexed his biceps. "You love my body."

"That I do," Billy said, reaching up and running his hands over Teddy's soft, smooth skin, feeling the hard muscles underneath. "Fuck, you're hot." Billy started tugging down Teddy's shorts. "Come on, let's see it."

Teddy took Billy's hands and pinned them to the ground. Looking into Billy's eyes, Teddy pressed his hips into Billy. "Yeah, you want this dick, don't you? Say it. Tell me you want my big baseball bat."

"I'm not saying that," Billy laughed. "I do want that dick just as much as you want my ass." Billy raised his head and pecked Teddy on the lips. "Quit playing around."

"Say it," Teddy said more intensely. "Say it, fag boy. Tell me you want my big dick. Tell me how you're going to be waiting back at my hotel room after I get that MVP so you can lick the sweat from my balls."

Billy pressed his crotch up into Teddy. "You're nasty. And I won't be in your hotel room waiting because I'll be busy, straight boy."

"Sucking every dick you can, I bet." Teddy leaned down for a kiss, but Billy turned his head at the last minute. "Fucker. What *are* you going to be doing?"

"I'm going to be a porn star." Billy gave Teddy a salacious grin. "You know I got the skills… or do you need reminding?"

Teddy pretended to think for a moment. "Hmm… I think I need reminding." Teddy ground his crotch into Billy. "Why don't you remind me?"

"Gladly." Billy tried to move his pinned arms, but Teddy refused to free them. "This is fun, but we need to get naked already."

"Come on Mr. Porn Star, you've got to build up the anticipation." Teddy buried his mouth in the crook of Billy's neck again.

Billy relaxed his body, enjoying the roughly sensual attack of Teddy's mouth. Teddy played the aggressive dom top role well, but Billy knew the truth. Teddy was a bottom pleaser, concerned with the guy with whom he was playing's pleasure more than his own. He couldn't climax until his willing partner did.

"Too many clothes," Teddy grumbled, finally releasing Billy from his grip. "Get naked."

"You've got to get off me." Billy playfully pushed Teddy off him. "What happened to building anticipation?" Billy pulled off his crop top and shimmed out of his shorts, his hard eight inches swinging up and thumping his slim stomach. "Or are we finally fast-forwarding to the good part?"

Teddy stood. Arrogantly, he looked down at Billy with his hands on his hips, thumbs in the waistband of his shorts. "Oh, we're still building anticipation." He

lowered his shorts just a little, so Billy could see the top of his black-trimmed pubic hair. "Say it," Teddy said, rocking his hips as he alternatively lowered one side while raising the other. "Say it, and I'll unleash the beast."

Billy got on all fours and began crawling toward Teddy. "I'm not saying it. Besides, you already unleashed the beast." Teddy laughed as Billy slowly stalked forward. "Now, give me that dick." Billy lunged forward, grabbing the bottom of Teddy's shorts before he could get away.

Teddy laughed, playfully struggling to keep them up before letting Billy win. "Finally," Billy huffed, sliding the shorts down Teddy's legs and freeing his nine inches. "Now, for my prize."

Billy caught Teddy's bouncing dick with his mouth, sucking on the head and swirling his tongue around the crown. Teddy moaned, staggering back just a bit. He put a steadying hand on Billy's shoulder, so he could step out of his shorts. Billy wouldn't give up his prize, taking more and more of Teddy into his mouth.

Billy sat back on his heels as he sucked Teddy down, running his tongue along the underside of the shaft and toying with the head. Billy took his time, enjoying the feel of Teddy in his mouth and with practiced skill, he swallowed Teddy whole, pressing his nose into Teddy's groin before pulling back and starting over again.

Teddy moaned, "God, Billy. Suck my big dick, suck it."

Billy moaned, increasing his pace. Each time he took Teddy down to the root, then moved back to play with the tip. He knew that Teddy liked to enjoy their time together, making it last until they were both covered in sweat and Billy's ass and jaw ached. Billy would miss this when Teddy left him to head off to school. He hoped Teddy would miss it, too.

"Fuck, Billy," Teddy panted. "You do have skills."

Teddy stepped back, pulling his cock from Billy's hungry mouth. He leaned down and caught Billy's mouth with his own before Billy could lunge at his dick again. He guided Billy until he fell onto his back. Covering Billy's body with his own, he wedged his legs between Billy's. Billy's legs spread for him as easily as melted butter.

Teddy sucked on Billy's tongue while Billy raked his nails across his bare back. He kissed his way down to Billy's pert nipple. Teddy's tongue circled the tiny brown nub, and then he bit it gently, causing Billy to gasp mid-moan. He flicked his tongue over the sensitive spot, then swirled his tongue once more.

"Teddy," Billy groaned through clenched teeth, fisting the blanket, "you know what that does to me." Teddy ignored him, swapping over to his other nipple. "Oh, my God, Teddy!" Billy called out, releasing the blanket grabbing Teddy's head. "Bastard," he hissed when Teddy rapidly flicked his tongue.

Moving down Billy's body, Teddy lazily drew scribbles on Billy's skin with his tongue. Billy thrashed and jerked, his skin exploding with tiny orgasms. Teddy moved down, running his tongue in circles around Billy's belly button before he moved down to Billy's

rock-hard cock. Billy looked down at Teddy who flashed him a devilish grin before taking the head of Billy's cock in his mouth.

Billy ran his hands through Teddy's curly mop of hair. "Teddy, fuck," Billy cried softly, fighting the urge to buck up into Teddy's throat. Teddy still had that annoying gag reflex that Billy had lost already. "Your mouth is so hot, Jesus."

Teddy's eyes met Billy's. He watched Billy's face intently as he slowly worked Billy's cock. Billy saw the intent in his blue eyes while Teddy nursed just the tip of his cock. Billy knew it was coming. Trying to catch his breath, the only thing Billy could do was lay there and enjoy it.

Teddy let go of Billy's cock, kissed the tip then snaked his tongue in a zigzag pattern down Billy's shaft, down past Billy's balls, along Billy's taint. He lifted Billy's legs up, pushing them back into Billy's chest, exposing Billy's sweet smooth hole.

Teddy blew a stream of cool air onto Billy's pucker, causing it to twitch with anticipation. He gave an appreciative whistle. Billy was just catching his breath, when Teddy leaned in and slowly ran his tongue around the tender skin. Billy closed his eyes and groaned, enjoying the tantalizing touch.

Billy wrapped his arms around the back of his legs and pulled them farther back, trying to spreading himself further for Teddy. "Eat my ass. Get it all nice and sloppy wet for your big dick," Billy ordered as Teddy fluttered his tongue over his pucker. Billy arched his back. "Fuck yes! I knew there was a reason I kept you around."

Teddy continued unabated at the playful jab, giving Billy's ass a light slap as punishment. He pressed his tongue into Billy's hole, relaxing the rosebud into opening. Billy groaned, feeling the tongue slowly work its way into him, then pulling back to run across his sensitive skin.

Billy knew what Teddy was doing… it was a battle of wills. Billy wanted Teddy in him. Teddy wanted in Billy, but only if Billy begged for his big bat. They had played this game for months now. Billy had yet to yield. It drove Teddy crazy, driving him to come up with more creative sexual teasing with which to torture Billy.

"Fuck you," Teddy growled, pulling back from Billy's cheeks and moving up to hook Billy's legs on his shoulders. "Say it." Teddy had one hand holding himself up. The other hand he had on his cock, rubbing it along Billy's spit-slick crack. "Come on… say it, and you'll get it."

"I'm going to get it no matter what. I can hold out a whole lot longer than you," Billy huffed, face flushed with desire. He could feel Teddy's cock making small circles over his hole, ready to pierce him.

"Ass. You'll say it one day," Teddy groaned, pressing into Billy.

Billy felt the stretch of Teddy's cock as it entered him. "I'm saving it as a farewell present."

"Then I'll never hear it." Teddy groaned at the feel of Billy's ass pressing flush to his groin. "… because I'm never letting you go."

Billy believed him, the promise sealed with a kiss as Teddy raised and lowered his hips. Billy hugged

9

Teddy close, careful not to dig his nails too deeply into Teddy's back. It was no small feat considering each antagonizing slow push and pull of Teddy's cock rubbing against that special spot inside of him.

Breaking the kiss, Teddy pressed his forehead to Billy's. "I love how my dick feels in you. Man, Billy, how you make me feel..." he said, his voice barely over a whisper.

"Me, too," Billy answered, too scared to say the words he actually meant. "Fuck me, Teddy. Fuck me, please."

Teddy crushed his mouth to Billy's one last time, then began his reckless assault on Billy's ass. As he pumped hard into Billy, sweat began to bead on Teddy's skin. Each forceful plunge into Billy brought him just a little closer to that grand finale. It was just out of reach, and they both knew why.

"Faster. Harder," Billy pleaded.

Teddy reared up on his haunches and pulled out of Billy. "Doggy," he snarled.

Billy quickly rolled over onto all fours, and he already missed the feel of Teddy inside him. Teddy spat on his own dick, then lined up with Billy's winking hole. They both groaned when Teddy sheathed his cock back into Billy. He gave Billy a few tentative poundings, and then went all-in. Gripping Billy's hips, Teddy pulled him back along his length while he thrust forward. Teddy was almost there. He could feel it screaming in his balls to be let out. He knew there was only one way he'd release.

He let go of Billy's hips and grabbed him by the shoulder. He pulled Billy back until he sat against

Teddy, back to chest. Teddy wrapped his arm around Billy's chest, holding him close. His other hand, Teddy spat in, slipping it around Billy till he found those hard eight inches. Billy turned his head, his mouth finding Teddy's.

The two kissed, sensual and needy. Teddy bucked up into him, bouncing Billy's cock through his hand. Teddy fucked Billy, and in turn, Billy fucked Teddy's hand. Teddy's other hand began flicking over his nipple. Billy began to whimper, his climactic detonation looming dangerously close.

Billy couldn't hold it back any longer. Sweat trickled down his temples. His legs were growing weak, and his body quivered with the impending surge. Billy broke the kiss but kept his lips close to Teddy's. "Teddy," Billy's voice trembled with the promise of pleasure. "I'm going to—" Billy started to say, but the words were cut off with a monstrous yell of pleasure.

Billy's ball drew up, and his cock throbbed in Teddy's hand as the first of many blasts exploded. He quaked from the rush of endorphins flooding his body. Teddy held him tight as he convulsed with every cock shot. Their lips met again, muffling Billy's cries. His hand covered in spunk, Teddy continued stroking Billy,

Teddy began to furiously thrust up into Billy. Billy, clenching from the orgasm, was as tight as when they began. Teddy's hips rigorously rocked back and forth, short quick jabs. He was there, and his cock unleashed a torrent inside Billy. He sucked hard on Billy's tongue, his grip on Billy almost as tight as the one Billy's ass had on his cock.

Teddy continued fucking Billy until they could hear the wet sound of sperm sliding in and out. They fell over onto their sides, Teddy spooning Billy, his cock wedged deep into his late-morning lover. Billy rested his head on Teddy's bicep as Teddy's other arm draped over him. Billy clung to that arm like a security blanket.

Teddy whispered sweetly, half asleep after the encounter, "I love you, Billy. I hope you know that. I love you. No matter what, you'll always be mine."

"I love you too, Teddy. I'll always be yours, and you'll be mine," Billy said back, trying to hide the elation he felt. Billy patted Teddy's hand.

They laid on the cum-speckled blanket, naked and entwined in each other's bodies under the shade of the old oak tree. The wind blew the summer heat over them as they slowly drifted off to sleep, two young men in love without a care in the world. Two young men who thought they knew it all but knew nothing.

"Hey man." Billy startled awake at the stranger tapping his shoulder. "You might want to roll over." Billy looked at the grinning man, confused. "Your flag is at full mast." Billy followed the man's eyes down to his crotch. "Not bad. Give me a call some time." The man pushed a piece of paper into Billy's hand before walking away to rejoin his friends.

Billy quickly rolled over, hiding his excitement. *Great*, Billy thought, trying to will the blood to flow

away from his dick. *I can't even go home and take care of this because I have a shoot tomorrow.*

Billy lay there, feeling the eyes of everyone on him for another ten minutes before he gathered up his stuff and headed back to his apartment. It wasn't that he was embarrassed at having an erection in public; in his line of work, the ability to do that was listed as a special skill on a resume. He was mad at himself for being so naive back then.

You'll always be mine. Billy repeated the words in his head. *As long as no one knows, right Teddy?*

13

ARE YOU WATCHING PORN?

JORDAN PRETENDED HE didn't hear the unmistakable sound of sex in the background while on the review call with his supervisor. There was no mistaking it, though … the moaning or groaning. The only thing missing was the thump of a bed hitting the wall. Luckily, his mic hadn't picked up the cheesy porn lines his neighbor shouted while he was doing his sexual gymnastics during that particular call.

"Jordan," his supervisor said, pausing the playback, "what's going on during this call?"

"We're reviewing the bill, and I'm explaining the charges," Jordan answered, pretending not to know what she meant. "We were just about to talk about upgrading their plan."

"Jordan." He knew by the tone of her voice that she picked up on the background sounds. "I'm not deaf. Are you watching…" she lowered her voice, as if the meeting was face-to-face instead of virtual, "…porn?"

Jordan sighed. There was no point in continuing the ruse. "I have a new neighbor," he began to explain. "He's, um…" Jordan sought the right description. A whore? No. A slut? No. Had more sex than a colony of bunnies? No. "… sexually popular."

"Uh, huh." His supervisor sounded uncomfortable, but at least Jordan hadn't slut shamed. "Well, I think you need to have a talk with him about how loud he and his…" it was her turn to struggle with the proper HR term, "…guest? Yes, guests are."

"I will," Jordan promised, wanting to end this conversation. Looking at the time, he found his way out. "I'm actually off now. Can we pick this up in our next coaching? I have to go. I have an appointment."

His supervisor didn't hide the annoyance of having her meeting cut short. "Yes, go ahead and clock out." Jordan masked the relief on his face. "Go to your appointment, and make sure you talk to your neighbor."

"I will," Jordan reiterated. "See you Monday." Jordan closed the window with his supervisor's face, then hung up the line before she could start babbling for another ten minutes, eating into his precious time off.

Clocking out and shutting down his work computer, Jordan leaned back in his chair. "How is he not shooting dust by now?" Jordan wondered aloud. "Or gaping like the Holland tunnel?"

Jordan listened to the sounds, trying not to get turned on. *Whatever he's doing, he's really enjoying it.* Jordan spun around in his chair and leaned forward, resting his elbow on his knees. *He's really enjoying it.*

Jordan suddenly felt guilty for listening. Getting up, he grabbed his phone and earbuds off his desk. Getting something to drink from the kitchen on his way to the living room, Jordan got comfortable on the couch. He needed to take a moment to decompress from his day.

It was the same thing, day in and day out. If he complained, the upper management would come back with the same tired oxymoron: every call is different, and everyone is taking the same calls. How could they be different, yet the same? Were they just passing the same call over and over till they talked to every representative in the company?

Of course there were the basic calls Jordan got that he had to bite his tongue on. "Why is my bill so high?" to which Jordan wanted to ask, "Have you even looked at your bill?" Or say, "You haven't paid us in three months." Then, there were the people who thought their phones were hacked. He wanted to explain to those people they weren't as important as they thought they were *to* be hacked.

Jordan closed his eyes, took a deep breath, and let out all the negativity of the day. He couldn't bring this into his art. He took a few more cleansing breaths, then opened his eyes to look at the black screen of his tablet that mocked him. It sat there, taunting him, calling him to pick it up and fail.

"Fuck you," Jordan spat out at the tablet. As if on cue, his neighbor moaned loudly through the walls. "Seriously?" Jordan rolled his eyes. "How is he not raw by now?" Jordan popped in his ear buds. *I'll talk to him tomorrow.* Jordan turned the music on his phone.

Music drowned out the sounds of sex seeping into his apartment. Picking up his keyboard off the side table, he let the music take him away. Connecting it to his tablet, Jordan opened the blank document that pleaded with him to paint it with his words, use it to bring to life the story that lay hidden inside him.

Jordan's fingers hovered over the keys, poised for action. At any moment now, it was going to happen. The words were going to come to him; he had to coax them out, entice them to come forth. He was in the mood; he just had to rise to the occasion. Then he could pump out his words all over the paper and finally feel satisfied.

"Fuck," Jordan said into the room, slamming himself back into the couch cushions. Pulling out his earbuds, he said louder than he intended to, "Will you just do it and get it over with!" Then he added, "Why won't you just come already?!"

The sex sounds Jordan had been ignoring stopped. He nearly jumped out of his skin when he heard pounding on the wall, then his neighbor's muffled shout of, "Rude!"

RIDING IN CARS WITH BOYS

BILLY INSTANTLY FELT guilty for yelling through the wall at his neighbor. He *was* being a little loud rehearsing his sex sounds for the shoot tomorrow; he could only imagine what his neighbor thought he was doing. Then, he thought of all the times he did that for his fan content and began laughing.

At least he knows I have a healthy sex life, Billy mused. *A* very *healthy sex life.*

Billy checked his phone, hoping that a miracle happened, that his mother acknowledged one of his many attempts to contact her. Even if it was a "leave me alone" or "stop," at least Billy would know she was reading his texts or listening to his voicemails.

She never did respond. She obviously still blamed him for what he never did. It hurt that his mother believed her leech of a boyfriend over him. It hurt, but he understood it. He knew he would have done the same thing, as horrible as it was. He was his mother's son. It's what she taught him to do.

It's what she did: put the men she loved ahead of everything and everyone else. If the men didn't love her, that was okay; they loved how easily she spread her legs for them and treated them like royalty, when they themselves were the equivalent of the bottom layer of trash in a ten-year-old landfill.

"It doesn't matter if a man loves a woman or not," his mother told him before it became obvious that Billy liked dicks, not chicks. "All a woman has to do is open her legs to get what she wants from a man."

Billy set his phone down on the nightstand. Climbing into his bed, he snuggled up to the gigantic stuffed bear. Back East, he had Carlos to cuddle with. He wished he could have brought Carlos with him, but Carlos needed to get his break with people who wouldn't take advantage of him. Billy trusted Dennis and Hunter to do that.

Billy had to settle for the stuffing and fabric of the giant stuffed animal. It wasn't the same as a warm body, but it was something to help deal with the loneliness. Billy grabbed his phone off the nightstand and took a quick selfie of himself curled up next to his stuffed animal.

His followers would like the cutesy picture of him. They would see he was happy and carefree, instead of sad and lonely. He lay his phone down and closed his eyes. He still remembered that horribly wonderful night that changed his life. He could still hear Bobby Lee's thick country accent.

He had arrived home from working his shift at the burger joint and immediately jumped in the shower to wash off the stench of sweat and burger grease.

19

Bobby Lee, his mother's current loser boyfriend, was in his usual spot on the couch watching television and drinking beer while his mother worked her second job to support him.

Billy had slipped into a new pair of skin-tight jeans and form-fitting graphic tee. Tonight he was headed to the Candy Shop. It took forty-five minutes to get there down an old country road, but it was better than driving an hour and a half to the one in the city. The Candy Shop's added bonus was it didn't check IDs.

Billy just finished styling his hair and was ready to head out, but Bobby Lee had other plans. Billy opened the door of the home's single bathroom to find Bobby Lee standing there waiting, smelling of cheap beer and cigarettes. Billy tried to move around the man, but Bobby Lee blocked him.

Billy huffed at him, annoyed. "What gives, Bobby Lee?" Billy avoided the man as much as possible. He saw the way Bobby Lee leered at him and he was certain his mother had as well. "I got to go. I'm meeting people," Billy lied.

"You're of those fags, right?"

Billy rolled his eyes at the question. "Yes, I'm gay. Can I go now?" Billy asked through clenched teeth.

Billy tried to get around the man, but he blocked Billy again. "Now, hold up a minute." Billy crossed his arms. "Your mama promised to care for my needs, but she's been working an awful lot lately." At this, Billy knew what Bobby Lee really wanted. "Now, that means she ain't been doing what she promised."

Billy's face twitched. He fought to force a smile instead of sneer. "You could get a job and help out. You know, instead of sitting on the couch all day drinking and smoking."

Bobby Lee thrust back his shoulders, trying to be intimidating. "Now, boy, don't you sass me. You know your mama hitched herself to my wagon for that settlement I'll be getting. If I ain't getting my needs taken care of here, well…"

"You'll get them taken care of somewhere else," Billy sighed. "Right, and she'll be pissed at me."

Billy hated the smug look on his face. "Exactly. So why don't you just get down on your sissy knees and put those pretty boy fag lips to good use?"

Billy gagged. "I'm not sucking your nasty dick. You need to shower. If I smell your nasty ass or your dick cheese, I'm biting off your dick."

Bobby Lee raised an arm to sniff his pit, showing the stained underarm. Billy didn't know how his mother could stand sharing a bed with this pig. "I guess I could use a shower. Fine." Bobby Lee stepped out of the way, allowing Billy to slip by. Bobby Lee grabbed his ass. "You'll be giving that up next, fag."

Billy swatted Bobby Lee's hand away. "Hurry up and shower." He moved out of arm's reach. "I've got plans tonight."

"The only plans you got to worry about is you sucking my big ol' dick." Bobby Lee laughed nastily, stepping into the bathroom. Shutting the door, he shouted, "That's what fags like you are good for, servicing men like me."

Billy rolled his eyes. He listened to the shower cutting on and then the splatter of water when Bobby Lee stepped in. Billy snatched his keys out of his room and rushed out the door. At least Bobby Lee would be clean when he realized Billy wasn't there anymore. Billy hoped his mother would appreciate him tricking Bobby Lee into showering.

That night Billy danced without a care in the world on the tiny dance floor. An hour into moving to the rhythmic beats, he pulled his shirt off and shoved it into his back pocket. He could feel the lustful leers of the men over his sweat-glazed body. He loved every minute of it.

It was just after twelve when he finally pulled himself away and headed to the water jug set up for those too cheap or broke to spend money on booze. Billy downed the first cup he poured for himself, then poured the second down his chest. The shockingly cold water pebbled his skin and garnered the attention of the few people who weren't already watching.

Billy noticed the three men sitting at a table in a corner, eyeing him. He knew who they were, even if they didn't know who he was. Everyone at the bar knew who they were. They were the Gay A's of this bar. The bar elite. Sure, that status meant nothing in the real world, but in this world, it was the ultimate status.

With a youthful confidence and a cocky smile that he didn't have the right to have, Billy swayed his hips as he strutted across the club to their table. Putting his hands on the table, Billy bent at the waist, arching his back dramatically and thrusting out his smooth toned chest.

Licking his lips, he said, "Hi, I'm Billy."

"That's nice. You can go now," the broad-shouldered man with a square jaw answered. With his pressed polo and khaki pants, he reminded Billy of the coach at his old high school who was forced to teach classes he didn't care about.

"Don't be rude, Joe," the man in the middle interjected. Billy liked his bad boy look, with his scattered tattoos on his bare arms. The man was lean and hard with sinewy muscle and black hair cut to the scalp—either for style, or to hide the obvious male pattern baldness.

The man leaned forward and stuck out his hand. "I'm Brett." Billy took Brett's calloused hand. "You've met Joe." Brett withdrew his hand and leaned back, putting his arm around their third. "This is my partner, Shadow."

Shadow leaned forward to take Billy's hand. Billy found his name ironic; his straw-yellow, short-blonde hair and his sunny bright smile did not depict the young man as dark as a shadow. "Hi, Billy. Care to join us?"

"Sure." Shadow got off the booth so Billy could slide in between them. Brett draped his arm over Billy's shoulder. Sliding back in the booth, Shadow rested his hand on Billy's inner thigh. "You guys sure are friendly," Billy joked.

"We sure are. Are you friendly, Billy?" Brett pulled Billy a little closer.

"Oh, I'm friendly. I'm real friendly." Billy slipped a hand between each of the men's legs.

Shadow's hand moved up to Billy's hardening crotch. "So are we. We're also adventurous. Would you like to get out of here and go on an adventure with us, Billy?"

"I…" Billy was about to turn them down, thinking he had bitten off more than he could handle, but the guffaw from Joe changed his mind. "I'd love to."

"Glad to hear that." Brett shot a look over at Joe. "You're driving."

After a little casual fondling and a death glare from Joe, the men were out the door. A little nervous about leaving his beat-up car, Brett assured Billy his car would be safe, and they'd bring him back after. That did little to ease the uneasy knots in Billy's stomach, but he let Shadow and Brett steer him to their black SUV.

Getting into the driver's seat, Joe grumbled something under his breath. Shadow gave Billy a coy smile, opening the back passenger door for Billy to slip into with Brett before he got in the front passenger seat.

Brett sat invitingly, slightly askew with an arm across the back of the seat and legs open wide. Joe started the engine, bathing the cabin into a short-lived darkness. Neon party lights illuminated the back seat in muted blue and white. Billy was more than a little impressed by the seemingly unnecessary extravaganza.

"We like to be watched," Brett said, pointing to the various cameras situated around the SUV's cabin. "A lot of people like to watch us."

"Okay. I don't mind." Billy, still shirtless, wasn't sure what he meant.

Brett gave him a salacious smile. "Good. Why don't you come over here and show me what your mouth can do?"

Bill returned that smile. "Gladly. I hope you can handle it."

"I think you're the one who needs to worry about handling it," Brett said. He let Billy slide up his body. "Give daddy a kiss."

Billy pressed his lips to Brett's. The kiss was tentative at first. Then, with one of Brett's hands going to the back of his head, the kiss turned carnal. Brett slipped his other hand down his back and down the back of his pants. Brett's hand cupped his bare cheeks. Billy pressed his body into Brett's, rubbing his hard crotch against his counterpart's.

Steadying his body with one arm, Billy slipped the other between him and Brett. With eager fingers, he popped open the button of his jeans and slid down his zipper, loosening his skin-tight jeans. Brett's middle finger slipped between Billy's mounds and brushed over his hole. With his eager humps into Brett, Billy's jeans worked their way down.

Brett reluctantly pushed Billy off him. "Fuck, I need you out of those jeans, and your mouth on my cock."

"Sounds good to me." Billy kicked off his sneakers and peeled off his pants.

"Damn," Brett said, pulling off his shirt, revealing more tattoos on his chest. "You're a big dick bottom."

Billy grinned at him, stroking his cock while Brett worked his pants off. "Come get your mouth on this."

Billy, lost in his sexual craving, moved between Brett's legs. His mouth surrounded Brett's long, ten-inch cock. He sucked most of Brett down before coming back up to make another attempt at getting those last few damned inches down. Brett rested his hand on the back of Billy's head, giving the illusion he was forcing Billy down.

Brett moaned, pushing his hips up into Billy's mouth. "He's got a mouth like a Hoover. You've definitely got to get some of this, Shadow."

Billy felt the car start to move, but he didn't care. Brett had reached behind him and was tapping a spit-wet finger at his hole. Billy got up on his knees on the seat, thrusting his ass up, making it easier for Brett to push his finger in. It took him a while, with Billy changing his angle of attack, but he eventually got all but an inch of Brett down.

Brett held Billy's head down in his lap. "Oh, fuck yeah. Get it all." Brett punched his cock up into Billy's throat. Billy tried to cough and sputter, but the cock wedged in his throat only allowed him to make gagging sounds. "Yeah, boy. Gag on that cock."

Brett let Billy off his cock, but only long enough for Billy to catch his breath before Brett had his cock slamming into his mouth again. This time Billy's gagging was less when he buried his nose into Brett's hairless groin. The next time was easier, and the time after that, Billy wasn't gagging any longer and was fucking his own throat with Brett's cock.

Brett laughed, pushing his finger into Billy's hole. "He's a quick learner. Oh, he's tight, too." Brett pushed a second finger in along with the first. "Of course, he won't be once I'm done."

Billy rocked his hips back into Brett's thrusting fingers. He squeezed and relaxed his hole, trying to prepare himself for Brett's hard cock. He had fucked in the backseats of cars before, but this was the first time he was having sex with an audience. He couldn't deny how turned on he was. The thrill of being caught in the woods with Teddy was hot, but an actual audience was exhilarating.

Brett moaned, taking his hand off the back of Billy's head to run it over his own chest. "Yeah, Billy. Fuck, that feels good."

Billy groaned. He was playing with Brett's cock now, running his tongue over the crown, running along his shaft as he sucked Brett down. He was loving this more than he expected, the audience and the recording. His own cock was harder than he could ever remember it being, and he was certain he was dripping a puddle of pre-cum on the leather seat below him.

Brett pulled his fingers from Billy's ass, and Billy off his cock. "Let me see that pretty hole of yours. Lean over the console." Brett maneuvered Billy to lean into the front over the center console, his ass on full display for Brett. "Fuck, that's a pretty hole." Brett ran his finger over Billy's puckering hole. "Looks sweet, too. Do you have a sweet hole, Billy?"

"Ye—" Billy's response was cut off by the press of Brett's tongue into him. "Oh, fuck," Billy gasped

as Brett made out with his hole. "Jesus." Billy gripped the center console. He looked over to see that Joe was ignoring him, but Shadow was watching with delight. Brett worked his tongue into Billy, getting him sloppy wet. "Fuck, eat that hole."

Brett gave his ass a slap, then spread his cheeks farther so he could go deeper. Billy was moaning loudly, not worrying about being heard. For the first time, he could be as loud as he wanted. He didn't have to worry about someone wandering the woods hearing Teddy and him. He didn't have to keep quiet in case a parent or sibling heard him while he was giving it up to one of the "straight" boys that just needed a bit of relief.

"I need that ass now," Brett growled, gripping Billy by the hips and pulling Billy back into his lap. "You ready for some cock in that ass?"

Billy's voice was filled with lust. "Yes. Give me that cock." He raised up, grabbing the seats in front of him for leverage. Brett positioned his cock at his hole. Billy slowly lowered himself onto Brett's cock. "Damn, you're big."

Billy's eyes rolled back in his head as the head of Brett's cock popped effortlessly into him. It was the next nine inches that Billy had to force his body to accept. Billy rose and fell little by little, pushing more of Brett into him. It was slow going, but Billy was going to do it. He'd prove to Brett and Shadow he was one of them.

Shadow reached back and put a small brown bottle under Billy's nose. He had the bottle under one of Billy's nostrils and his fingers closing the other. "Here, inhale. Take a deep whiff and hold it." Billy did. He got lightheaded. "Now, exhale." Billy did as instructed. Shadow had Billy repeat it with the other nostril before retreating back to the front.

Billy's head was swimming. His body grew warm, and he could swear he saw sparks of light in his vision. Brett guided him back down into his lap. Miraculously, he was sitting in Brett's lap. Billy rested there, amazed that there was no noticeable pain with all ten inches in him. He had to find out what was in that little brown bottle.

When Billy rested there a moment too long, Brett nudged him up. With his hands on the front seats for support, Billy bounced up and down on Brett's cock. Brett met his bounces, thrusting his dick up. Billy couldn't go fast enough, the euphoric sensation driving him. He caught a glimpse of his sex-crazed face in the rearview mirror, then he noticed the worried eyes of Joe watching him.

"On your back," Brett snarled, moving Billy to lay across the back seat. Billy's head was on the arm rest and Brett had his legs in the air. Brett said, sliding back into Billy, "Jack your cock. I want to see you cum. Pump that big dick!"

Billy did, unable to vocalize the words swirling around in his head. Brett was pumping his cock into him mercilessly. He stroked his cock, slowing down only when Brett randomly leaned down to kiss him. Billy could feel it, that cataclysmic orgasm building. He didn't want to shoot his load, but he couldn't stop.

Billy shouted, arching his back up off the seat as the white ropes of cum splattered across his smooth flat stomach and pooled in his belly button. "Fuck!

Damn!" Billy jerked, blasting load after load till his cock began going soft.

Brett pulled out of Billy and put an arm on the door behind Billy. Brett's other hand was stroking his own cock. "Hell, yeah." Then it hit him, Brett's load. It landed on him, the two different shades of white mixing on Billy's body. Brett leaned down and kissed Billy, careful not to get any evidence of their tryst on him. "That was hot."

Brett returned to his seat, leaving Billy recovering on his. "Pass the wipes," Brett asked. Shadow passed back a package of baby wipes. Brett started cleaning himself up. "You know, Billy, you got a hot little body, and you're not bad in the sack." Billy just stared at Brett, his mind still not realizing what just happened. "If you ever need some extra cash, I think we could find you some good work."

"Um, sure. Thanks," Billy said confused, taking some baby wipes and cleaning himself up. The SUV stopped and Joe cut off the engine. "What time is it?"

"One," Joe's gruff voice answered.

Billy scrambled to sit up and start dressing. "Damn, I need to get back to my car and head home. How long till you can take me back to my car?"

Billy was confused at the men's laughter. "We never left." Shadow winked at Billy. "We drove in a circle." Shadow thrust his phone back at Billy. "Here, call yourself from my phone so we have each other's numbers." Billy, eager to get out of the back seat, did so without question. "Give us a call. Brett got to play with you, and I want my chance."

Billy smiled, slipping on his pants. "Sure. Look, I really got to go. My mother will kill me if I'm out too late."

"How old are you?" Joe's accusatory question came from the front.

Billy answered, slipping on his shoes, "I just turned eighteen. Thanks for the fuck." Billy leaned in and gave Brett a quick peck on the lips. "I'll be in touch, I promise." Billy opened the door and raced out to his car. In his car, he was all too aware of the scent of sex which covered his body.

Starting his car, he looked at the SUV and smiled. *Yeah, I did that,* he thought proudly before pulling out of the parking lot and into the night. *Man, that was fucking hot.* Billy could feel his dick filling again. "Not now. We got to get home," he scolded his crotch.

DO YOU KNOW WHO YOU ARE?

JORDAN PICKED UP his phone and opened his Twitter. He sat on his couch, scrolling through his feed. He told himself it was for inspiration, but it was actually a distraction to keep him from feeling like shit for not writing anything. He had wasted half a day with only a blank screen to show for it, a blank, haunting screen of which he grew tired, and yet he couldn't take his eyes off.

Jordan paused scrolling through his feed when he found one of his favorite porn stars. The star posted a selfie curled up with a giant teddy bear. The picture wasn't sexual or suggestive, but Jordan's mind went to those places. He wished he could be that bear.

Jordan knew it was foolish. He had short black hair that stuck every which way, no matter how much product he used. His face—his only smooth feature— was round and full to fit with his cub, stocky body. Fit and sexy guys like Billy didn't go for guys like Jordan.

Guys like Billy didn't talk to the stocky guys—let alone look at them.

There were guys that liked Jordan, but it wasn't reciprocated. They woofed or growled at him. He knew it was to show their appreciation or interest in him, but he just felt weird about it. He didn't know how to respond any other way than to say, "Thanks." He just wanted a normal, down-to-Earth guy with whom he could cuddle and watch bad television.

Jordan liked the picture. *What I wouldn't give to be that teddy bear. Of course, I wouldn't know what to do if I was that teddy bear...*

The knock on his door startled Jordan out of his thoughts. "Coming!" he yelled, wondering who it could be. All his friends knew he worked until seven, and he hadn't told any of them he was taking a half-day off today, not that they visited him often anyway. "Who is it?"

Jordan rose, mentally cursing, when the voice on the other side shouted through the door, "Your neighbor!"

Jordan wasn't good with conflict, despite his job. Making his way to the door, Jordan prepared himself to be cursed at, punched, or both. Their little inadvertent exchange had apparently bothered his neighbor more than he expected. Now, he had to deal with an angry testosterone-driven gorilla, or a huffy hypersexual twink.

What he wasn't expecting was the golden-blonde-haired, youthful, and angular face of the smooth, toned body he was crushing on moments ago. If he could have moved, he would pinch himself, or search

his apartment for the lamp to get his other two wishes. This couldn't be happening.

"Hi, I'm your loud neighbor, Billy." Frozen, Jordan stared at the outstretched hand. His gesture ignored, Billy began waving the hand in front of Jordan's face. "Hello? Anyone in there?" Billy put his hand on his waist. "Are you okay?"

"You're Billy. My neighbor," Jordan finally managed to get out.

Billy's eyes darted left, then right, before looking back at Jordan. He gave Jordan a questioning look. "Yeah, that's what I said. Do you need me to call someone for you?"

"You're Billy. My neighbor," Jordan repeated dumbfounded, adding, "the porn star."

Billy smiled brightly. "Oh, you've seen my work. I wouldn't call myself a star. A porn actor, but not a *star*."

Jordan was in awe, barely able to form coherent sentences. "Twitter. Your picture. I liked it. It was cute. The picture."

Billy felt honored someone was fanboying over him. "Thanks, but do you need to sit down or something?"

"I, uh, need to talk to you. About the noise," Jordan said, finally managing a coherent thought.

"Maybe you should invite me in? Maybe give you a chance to recover from meeting me?" Billy suggested.

"Yes, I'm sorry. Come in. Have a seat anywhere," Jordan blurted out, excited, and stepping aside to let in Billy.

"Nice place. I'm sorry I haven't come over and introduced myself sooner," Billy said, looking around before sitting on the sofa.

"That's okay. You're Billy," Jordan replied, in awe. He returned to his place on the sofa, all too aware the only thing separating him from Billy was a couch cushion. "You're a busy man, or so I've heard through the walls."

"Yeah, that's not what it sounds like," Billy replied, actually embarrassed about what he was about to admit. "That was me practicing my sex sounds ... for the most part."

"That was you *practicing*? Wow. You were really convincing. My supervisor thought I was watching porn. I told her you were a whore." Jordan blanched at his comment. "I'm sorry. I didn't mean to call you a whore. I know sex work is real work. Please, don't hate me."

Billy put a comforting hand on Jordan's knee. "Relax. I've been called worse and with a lot more hate. How did your supervisor hear me?"

"I, uh, work in customer service from home. My supervisor was reviewing a call with me, and your moaning could be heard in the background," Jordan admitted sheepishly. "She told me to talk to you about your sounds."

Billy snapped his fingers. "Okay, easy fix. I just won't practice my sounds or film content in my apartment when you're working. When do you work?"

Jordan answered, wincing, "Ten to seven. Monday through Friday. That doesn't give you too much time during the day to do your, uh... stuff."

Billy shrugged. "Actually, I start shooting for studios tomorrow, so I won't be home those days. If I do fan content at home, I can do it around your schedule."

Billy gave Jordan a mischievous grin. "It might mean you falling asleep to me screaming, 'Fuck me! Suck that dick! Yes! Ugh, yes!'"

Jordan's eyes went big, then narrowed at Billy. "You're fucking with me, aren't you?"

Billy leaned back into the sofa, a smug, shit-eating grin on his face. "Yup. Now that we got all that out the way," Billy sat back up and stuck his hand out, "I'm Billy. And you are?"

Jordan looked at the hand, dumbfounded, before he realized he hadn't given Billy his name. Taking Billy's hand, he said, "I'm so sorry. I'm an ass. I'm Jordan."

"Pleasure to meet you. So, what do you have going on there?" Releasing Jordan's hand, Billy nodded to the tablet.

Jordan looked at the bane of his existence, the white screen with the blinking cursor daring him to type a letter, any letter. "Nothing." Jordan reached over and laid the terrorizing tablet face down. "Just nothing."

"Uh, huh." Billy looked at the offending tablet, then back at Jordan. "Aren't you supposed to be working? Am I interrupting your lunch or something?"

"No, I took half a day off to…" Jordan sighed. "I took half a day off."

"Okay, if we're going to be friends, you can't keep stuff from me." Billy saw his words shocked Jordan. "We *are* going to be friends, right? Or are we going to be the type of neighbors that just nod and wave at each other?"

"You want to be my friend?" Jordan asked in disbelief. Since he started working from home, he had lost

touch with most of his work friends, and he rarely got to see his actual friends anymore, since they were all settled down in relationships or enjoyed the bar scene more than Jordan. "Me?"

"Yeah, you." Billy felt a little embarrassed about what he was about to admit. "You know, I just moved here, and I don't really know anyone who isn't in the industry. It would be nice to have a regular friend that I could bitch to." When the silence lingered too long between them, Billy added hastily, "That is, if you want to be friends."

"Yeah, totally," Jordan said quickly, realizing Billy was being serious. "I would be honored to be your friend. I mean, you're *Billy*."

"Okay, first rule," Billy laughed. "You've got to stop saying my name like I'm the Queen of England. I am a queen, but not of a country. I'm a regular guy just like you, who you happened to see naked and having sex."

"Okay, I'll stop," Jordan chuckled. "It's just that you're…"

"Billy. I know," Billy finished. "Alright, now rule two. Tell me why you took off and what you were doing on that tablet." Jordan cringed. "I promise I won't judge."

Jordan clenched his teeth, debating. Billy's imploring eyes finally got to him. "Fine. I'm an aspiring writer, and I took half a day off my customer service job to write." Jordan took the tablet off the table and unlocked it. He showed the blank screen to Billy. "Obviously, I've failed."

"You haven't written anything?" Billy asked.

37

"I've written stuff before," said Jordan, placing the tablet on the table. "I just haven't written anything lately."

"Okay…" Billy drew out the word. "Then, why are you an *aspiring* writer instead of a writer?"

"Because I haven't published anything. Well, except on my blog, but not where anyone important will ever see it," Jordan hated admitting.

"But you have written?" Billy asked to clarify.

"Yes, but nothing published," Jordan answered.

"Then, why are you aspiring? I mean, you've written. That means you're a writer." Billy's words confused Jordan.

"I…" Jordan didn't know how to answer the question. He stared down into his lap. "I just am, okay?"

Billy put a hand on Jordan's knee. "Look at me." Jordan reluctantly looked up at Billy. "You *are* a writer; you just have to admit it to yourself."

"I just don't feel like a writer. I think my stuff is good, but if it were, wouldn't I be published by now?" Jordan asked, looking back down in his lap.

Billy pulled out his phone. "It takes time, effort, and connections." He looked for the picture he posted which Jordan had "liked." He scrolled through the silenced notifications until he found the one that had to be Jordan. "Come here, we're taking a selfie."

Billy pulled Jordan into a side-hug and quickly snapped a picture. "Come on. Smile." Billy deleted the picture before taking another. "Better." Billy looked at the picture and quickly posted it on his feed, tagging Jordan in it.

Jordan's phone went off. "What did you do?" He grabbed his phone and opened his Twitter. "What did you do?" He repeated seeing the post. He looked at Billy then read aloud, "My new bestie doesn't think he's a writer. I say that he is. Check out his profile and read some of his stuff, and don't forget to show my new bestie some love."

Billy grinned smugly, and Jordan's phone immediately started sounding off with notifications. "You're welcome. Oh, you may want to silence that for a day or so." Jordan stared at his phone as notification after notification popped up on his screen. "So, new bestie, do you want to grab something to eat? Maybe catch a movie?"

Jordan looked wide-eyed at Billy. "Seriously? You did this, and now you want to do dinner and a movie?"

"Order in and stream? Okay, it was a bit much, but … go big, or go home?" Billy asked timidly.

Jordan looked back at his phone. "My phone is blowing up. What if they hate my stuff? What if they read what I wrote and tell me what I already know?" Jordan closed his eyes. "That I'm not any good."

Billy took Jordan's phone out of his hand and sat it on the table. "Okay, this weekend is you and me. We'll order some take out, stream a movie, and give each other facials." Jordan gawked at Billy. "Not *that* kind of facial. Then, tomorrow you're coming with me to my shoot."

"Your shoot? What shoot?" Jordan asked, confused.

Billy patted Jordan's leg. "I'm filming a scene tomorrow, and you're going to be my special guest. I think you need to be around your own kind."

"Porn people?" Jordan raised an eyebrow.

"Well, yeah, but creative people. What are you in the mood for? Chinese? Pizza? Burgers?" Billy picked up his phone.

THE ONLY REGRET

JOE SAT IN his old, stained recliner. The broken, worn chair was the only one in the house in which he felt comfortable. He spent most of his days and nights in that chair, mainly because it was too much of a struggle to get in and out of it. Most nights he fell asleep in it, not having the energy to make it upstairs to his room.

Once a day, a nubile young thing visited to drag him out of the chair to wash off his filth, make sure he took his medicine, and ate something warm. The muscular nurse was nice to look at, though he was achingly straight, not that Joe could do much more than look in his current condition.

Fearful of the truth for years, he ignored the doctors and refused to get the tests which would have caught the cancer early. By the time he finally relented, it was too late. He lived in an empty house which was falling apart around him, and an aggressive cancer was slowly destroying his body and his finances.

The precariously stacked final notices screamed at him from the coffee table. He had stopped opening them. There was no money for them; there wasn't any money for his faithful nurse, William, who still came despite not being paid. The man was a saint, never once asking Joe about the money he owed.

The sound of movement above him brought Joe out of his self-pity. There was no mistaking the creek of cautious footsteps above him trying to be quiet. Joe was familiar with the skitter of claws from the occasional curious squirrel or raccoon that found its way to the second floor. This wasn't a squirrel or raccoon. This was definitely the sound of a person lurking upstairs.

"Probably another damn meth-head thinking they found an easy score," Joe grumbled, setting the recliner upright. With considerable effort and cane in his hand, Joe rocked until he launched himself up onto unsteady feet. "Goddamn bastards can't even wait until I'm dead."

With his arm trembling from the weight of his body, Joe hobbled slowly from the recliner to the bottom of the stairs. Anything of worth up there had been sold long ago: the family antiques, his mother's jewelry, his father's diamond tie clip and matching cuff links. If he hadn't invested so heavily in Brett's failed porn site, he probably could have held onto them a bit longer.

Joe took a deep breath, preparing himself for the daunting task. With a steadying grip on the banister and his cane, he thrust himself up the first step, and then the next. The person upstairs was unabashedly

being loud now, knocking things over, and smashing things onto the floor.

Angered by the blatant disrespect for his things, Joe forced his body to continue. His arms and legs were wobbly from the exertion, and his breathing quickened. He needed to pause and rest to let his body catch up with his intentions, but each new crash of something hitting the floor or wall drove him further.

Three steps shy from the top, a shadowy figure appeared. Joe squinted trying to identify the intruder. "Get the fuck out of my house," Joe snapped with venom. When the figure didn't move, he shouted, "Get the fuck out of my house!"

Joe didn't see it coming, or he would have prepared for it. The force of the stranger's foot into his chest sent Joe flying back and crashing into the stairs before tumbling down. He wasn't sure if the cracking and snapping he heard was his own brittle bones or the splintering wood of the stairs. Pain exploded through his body.

He landed with an unceremonious thump at the bottom, the acrid taste of copper in his mouth. He willed his body to move, but it was too battered and abused to obey. He knew this was his time. This was the end for him, and he was okay with that.

He expected to be gripped by fear, to cry sobs of grief as the life slowly left his body. Instead, he felt a surge of peace. He wasn't even angry at the unknown person who had sent him flying down the stairs to his death. The intense pain faded away, replaced with a euphoric bliss.

43

Nothing mattered anymore. Not the bills that were left unpaid on his coffee table. Not the judgmental looks of the people in town whenever they saw him over the years. None of that mattered now as he drowned slowly in his blood. All that mattered now was his diminishing pain, and he'd never have to feel it again.

The boot of his salvation appeared in his blurred vision. Joe wondered if the owner would kick him for good measure, or spit on him for spite. The person just stood over him, talking to someone that wasn't there. The unknown person's voice was deep and resonating and undeniably male.

The voice said with clinical emotion, "May you burn in Hell for what you did to me."

Joe gurgled as his body tried to cough up the blood filling his lungs. He watched the booted feet move away. At least he wasn't dying alone. His only regret was William would find his body on Monday. The sweet nurse did not deserve that, but there was nothing he could do about it now.

Joe closed his eyes and said a silent prayer to a God he abandoned long ago. The darkness surrounded his consciousness, absorbing what light there was left in him. His journey was finished. Now, it was on to the next adventure. He hoped William wouldn't be too upset when he found Joe's lifeless body.

6

TIME TO PAY THE RENT, BOY

BILLY WAS UNCHARACTERISTICALLY nervous. He wanted to think it due to always being nervous during shoots, but that was a lie. These shoots came naturally to him. He loved being naked, and sex was second nature to him; ever since he was born, he had pretended to be someone he wasn't.

It was the *fantasy* of Billy that people wanted, and that's what he gave them. Billy, the good son. Billy, the secret fuck. Billy this, or Billy that. Porn was just a way for Billy to be someone everyone else wanted and never had to admit he didn't really know what *he* wanted.

Jordan was the real reason he was nervous. He pretty much forced Jordan to be his friend, which he hoped Jordan didn't regret, and he had fun with Jordan last night watching a movie and eating take-out. He got to be Billy for a moment, whoever that was.

Billy looked over to his co-star, Colton, who was pure muscle. He had perfectly styled, silvery-black hair, cut close on the sides with his the longer top locks strategically combed to one side. With his silvery-blue eyes and carefully manicured scruff along his chiseled chin and cheeks, Billy understood why he was such a fan favorite.

This was Billy's first time working with him, but he knew from pictures and videos that underneath the suit Colton now wore were bulging arms, a broad, defined chest, and washboard abs shaded by his dark body hair, on which you could scrub your laundry. He had thick, powerful thighs that could crack walnuts and his crowning jewel: an eight-inch, thick cock.

Colton gave Billy a reassuring smile. Earlier, they read through the script together, giving Billy a glimpse of the trademark personality for which Colton was known. With him, it wasn't an act. The fun, personable guy he showed on his social media was the same one right here, right now. Billy hoped he did the same on his social media.

It was time now to transform himself into the role he knew all too well. Billy wondered if he was being typecast—that somehow they knew his past, and when he started out on this path, it was necessary for Billy to do something like this in order to keep food on the table not only for himself, but for the other Country Boyz as well.

Colton stepped through the set door, carefully closing it behind him. It was time to sell the fantasy. "Honey, I'm home!" Colton called out, loosening his tie as he roamed the tiny set. "Baby, are you here?" Colton pretended to listen for a voice which wasn't coming before picking up the scrap of paper and reading it aloud for the online audience. "I had to run errands. I won't be home till late. Kisses."

Billy counted to ten before knocking on the door. In the split-second before Colton opened the door, Billy transformed into his character. Pulling from his past experience, Billy burst through the door and past Colton. Billy caught the sudden surprise in Colton's eyes at his sudden change in demeanor.

"So, this is where you live? It's nice," Billy said, walking around in jeans that hung low around his waist and were begging to be cut off. The shirt he wore fit his body perfectly.

Colton grabbed his arm, but Billy shook it off. "What the fuck are you doing here? Did anyone see you? You need to go before my husband comes home." Colton's voice was filled with panicked anger.

Billy made a show of popping his tongue. He lifted up his fist, raising a finger as he answered each question. "One, I need money. Two, I don't know, and I don't care. Three, not until I get my money."

Colton grabbed Billy by the arm. "I'm not giving you shit. Now get your ass out of here before I call the cops."

Billy yanked his arm away from Colton. "Go ahead, call the cops. I'm sure your neighbors would love the scene I cause," Billy threatened, putting a hand to his throat in an elaborate show. "He wants me arrested because he refuses to pay me for all the nastyyyy…" Billy drew out the word, "sex he had with me! You should hear the nastyyyy," again Billy drew out the word, "sick things he had me do that he now refuses to pay me for!"

"Keep it down," Colton said through clenched teeth, putting a hand over Billy's mouth. "The neighbors will hear you." Colton removed his hand to reveal Billy's self-satisfied grin. "Fine, you want money." Colton yanked out his wallet from his back pocket and pulled out some fake bills. "Here, take this, and get the fuck out of my house."

Billy snatched the bills from his hand. "Thank you very much. Now that I know where you live," Billy made a show of looking around, "and see all your nice things, I think you can afford to give me more next time."

"Fuck you. You're not getting any more money out of me," Colton spat out.

"We'll see. Until next time." Billy grinned, shoving the bills into the back pocket of his almost too-tight jeans.

Colton grabbed Billy's arm when he tried to leave. "Where do you think you're going? You're a whore, and I just paid you. I expect something for my money." Billy looked Colton in the eyes. He saw his own fake lust reflected back.

Billy hesitated a minute before pulling away. "What do you think you're doing?" Billy's hand clenched into a fist, ready to strike. He unfurled his fingers when he caught a glimpse of Jordan and remembered this was all an act.

Colton shot back on cue. "I'm going to get what I paid for. You didn't think you'd take my money and run, did you?"

"Yeah, I did." Spreading his legs wide to show off his bulging mound, Billy leaned back against a rented set table. Billy grabbed his own crotch. "Is this what you want? My cock down your throat? My balls bouncing against your chin?"

"I paid for it," Colton said, stepping in close. Billy put a hand to Colton's chest and gently pushed him back. "Give it to me."

"Fine," Billy laughed, "strip." Colton quickly pulled off his tie. Billy felt the past rush over him. "No," and Colton stopped with Billy's impromptu line. He waited to see where Billy was going with it. "You can do it better than that. Do it sexy for me … nice and slow." Billy licked his lips. "Make me want you."

Colton briefly glanced at the director who motioned him to go on. "You know you want this," Colton teased as he slipped off his jacket, then began slowly unbuttoning his shirt before gliding it off and revealing the muscular chest outlined by his trimmed chest hair.

Colton kicked off his shoes, then undid his pants. "You didn't come here for the money. You came here for me." Colton let his pants fall to the floor, revealing the ample pouch of his red bikini briefs. "You wanted more of this, the best you'll ever have."

Billy laughed an almost cynical laugh, "No, I wanted the money, but you wanted this…" Billy pulled the hem of his too-tight shirt up and off. He was a bit surprised he was able to without the fabric tearing. Tossing the shirt aside, Billy grabbed his crotch, "And this."

"You're an arrogant prick," Colton spat at Billy. They were totally off script now, but Colton went with it.

Billy wasn't deterred by the sudden change in tone. "Get on your knees," Billy ordered. When Colton didn't immediately obey, Billy added more forcibly, "Now." Colton dropped to his knees. "Good boy," Billy said, patting Colton on the head. "Now, tell me how much you want my cock."

"I want your cock," Colton said, almost too soft to hear. He looked up at Billy, then said louder, with more passion, "I want your big, fucking juicy cock!"

Billy stepped forward. He ran his hand through Colton's hair to the back of his head. "Yeah, you want my cock sliding into that tight ass of yours, don't you?" Billy pulled Colton into his crotch. "Say it."

Colton shouted into Billy's crotch. "I want you to fuck my tight ass! I want you to split me in half with that big dick of yours!"

Billy pushed Colton back off his crotch. Licking his lips, he began undoing his pants. "I don't think you want it bad enough. You better be glad I'm horny." Billy stepped out of his shoes, then shoved his pants down and off. His nearly ten inches swung out at Colton. "Suck it," Billy ordered. "Now!"

Colton moved forward on his hands and knees to the jutting cock. He looked up at Billy briefly before taking the flared head of Billy's cock into his mouth. His tongue danced over the tip while he took down a few more inches. This wasn't good enough for the Billy who was there right now.

"I said suck it, not play with it. You wanted that dick, and now you're going to get it." Billy put a hand to the back of Colton's head. With his grip firm but gentle, Billy thrust his hips back and forth, slamming his cock down Colton's throat.

Colton went with it, letting Billy use his mouth. Billy's ten inches easily slid down Colton's throat. He pretended to cough and sputter the few times Billy let him gasp for air, then willingly let Billy face-fuck him again.

Billy looked down the practice-perfect arch of Colton's back to the voluptuous ass barely covered by the thin strip of red fabric. The impulse took over. Bending over, Billy ran his hand down Colton's back into the skimpy underwear. He slipped his middle finger between Colton's firm, muscled ass and stroked his hole.

Hearing Colton's genuine moan, Billy reared back. "I'm going to fuck that ass good," Billy promised and pulled his cock from Colton's hungry mouth. Billy leaned down and kissed Colton hungrily before moving behind him. Dropping down to his knees, Billy pulled Colton's underwear down around his thighs. "Such a nice ass." Billy put his hands on the taut buttocks and spread the cheeks.

Billy admired the exposed pink hole ringed with tiny black hairs. He gave Colton's ass a hard smack, leaving a brief red handprint. "And a pretty hole," he said as his fingertips dug into Colton's ass. Colton gasped from Billy's tongue slashing wildly. "Fuck, yeah," Billy moaned.

Colton pushed back, his unrehearsed moans and groans escaping his lips, "Damn, fuck." Colton's body shuddered while he spoke. "Eat my hole," Colton

begged. He looked back at Billy smothering himself in his ass. "Keep that up and you might get a bonus."

"I'm getting my bonus now. Time to split you open," Billy said, getting up on his knees and rubbing his cock along Colton's spit-slick crack. Billy pushed cautiously into him. The head of his cock sank easily into Colton. He waited there, letting Colton get used to his cock's invasion.

"Like a hot knife through butter." With his hands on Colton's hips, Billy pushed in. Slowly he sank until he was balls deep. "Damn, that's nice."

Colton rolled his shoulders. He growled, rocking slightly back and forth on Billy's cock. "Fuck my ass. Fuck me."

Taking a firm grip on Colton, Billy pumped his cock in and out. Billy pulled out until just the head of his cock was in Colton, then thrust back in. Colton's body rocked back and forth bouncing off Billy's hips. Billy's nostrils flared with the intensity of the moment while Colton's eyes glazed over with pleasure.

Billy slammed hard into Colton, knocking him to the floor. Billy landed on top of the massive muscular body. Rolling onto their sides, Billy lifted Colton's leg up. "Oh, yeah that ass missed this dick, didn't it?" Billy asked, rabbit-humping Colton. "I know my dick missed this ass."

Colton grunted, working his underwear off his legs. "Yeah, I missed that dick. I missed that dick so much."

Billy pulled out and let Colton fall onto his back. He took Colton's ankles in his hands and held them up in the air. "I'm going to come back and fuck you in front of your man." Billy pushed his cock all the way in then pulled all the way out. "What do you think about that?" Billy pushed all the way in and wiggled his hips for emphasis.

"He can't know. Please, don't tell him," Colton pleaded, stroking himself.

"Oh, he's going to know. I'm going to cum all over your cheating face." Billy pistoled his cock into Colton.

Colton let out a groan, his hand moving rapidly over his cock. "Oh, fuck!" Colton arched up as his cock blasted across his lightly furred belly and chest. "Ugh, fuck, ugh!" Colton shouted, his body reverberating with his orgasm.

When Colton's eruption and tremors subsided, Billy pulled out. Letting Colton's legs fall, he moved to kneel beside Colton's euphoric face. Billy furiously jacked his cock until his cock detonated, shooting plumes of liquid, white ropes out to splatter across Colton's face.

Billy grunted with his body shakes, milking the last drips from his cock to fall onto Colton's thin red lips. His mind lost in the intensity of his climax, Billy looked down at the grinning face splattered with his spunk. It wasn't until Colton said, "Your roleplay fantasies are getting intense," that Billy remembered where he was.

"You enjoy them. At least the neighbors didn't complain this time." Billy smiled, slipping back into himself and alongside Colton.

"Fuck the neighbors. Can I have my money back now?" Colton asked, putting his arms around Billy.

Billy put his hand on Colton's heaving chest. "Nope. You've got to earn it back."

Colton kissed Billy. "Sounds good to me."

HEARTACHE TO HEARTACHE

BILLY HAD JORDAN drive them home. He had faked his way through the close-up shoots and shower with Colton. The director, pleased with the work, privately told Billy he didn't appreciate the ad-lib. Colton loved it, saying it felt real, raw, and probably one of the most intense scenes he'd ever done.

Billy hated making Jordan leave when he was having a good time talking to everyone but was grateful Jordan recognized the need to leave on his face. The scene stirred up memories with the Country Boyz for Billy, memories from when he was someone who extorted money for his tricks.

Jordan took the keys without question and drove them home without saying a word, letting the music from the radio fill the silence between them. Billy stared out the window and pondered his past. The night when Bobby Lee had propositioned him started a domino-effect on his life, beginning the path that led him here.

Billy inhaled deeply. Closing his eyes, he remembered the morning after Bobby Lee, waking up in his bed without a care in the world. That was the day he first learned not everyone who said they loved you really did. He learned that difficult lesson not once, but twice, as if God wanted to drill that lesson into him.

That same morning, he had slipped into a pair of sweatpants and headed to the kitchen with a goofy smile plastered on his face. His mother sat at the kitchen table, the one-handed grip on her coffee cup almost hard enough to shatter it. The other held a cigarette between two fingers, burnt halfway down with an ash waiting for the right moment to fall.

"Good morning. Start smoking again?" Billy asked his mother, walking straight to the refrigerator. She said nothing as Billy pulled out a carton of orange juice. He poured himself a glass and asked casually, "Where's Bobby Lee? I didn't see him in his usual spot."

His mother's calm voice quivered with anger. She ashed her cigarette into an empty beer can on the table. "Sit down, Billy. We need to talk."

Billy sat opposite her. "Okay, what about?"

She eyed Billy. She took a long, hard drag on her cigarette before dropping the butt into the can. She exhaled the smoke, and with nothing else to do with her hand, began clacking her nails on the table. The silence between them grew taut.

Right as Billy was about to speak, she did. "Bobby Lee told me what you did last night. How could you, Billy?" her tone accusatory.

Billy laughed. "Go to a bar? What's the big deal?"

Her clacking hand turned into a fist and slammed the table. "No! I'm talking about propositioning Bobby Lee. Trying to sleep with your mother's boyfriend? How could you?!" Billy gaped in surprise. Billy didn't know what to say. "Well?"

Billy's next words came out with venom and anger. "I did not proposition that couch-slug. He told me I needed to take care of him because you weren't!"

"Billy…"

He could tell she believed him but didn't want to. Billy felt the point of the dagger press into his heart at her next words. "You're eighteen now. I don't want to have to worry about you pushing yourself on my boyfriends."

Billy trembled with both fear and pain and said, "I would never. He's lying and you know it."

"It's time you went out and lived your own life… and I lived mine." She wouldn't meet his eyes.

"Mom. Don't," Billy's voice cracked.

His mom continued, unwavering, "Bobby Lee is at his sister's. I want you and your things gone by the time he gets back."

"Mom, I'm your son," Billy pleaded, watching her rise from the table.

"I have to go shopping," she stated as she walked to the door, not looking at him. She paused in the doorway, still not looking back. "You're a smart kid. You'll make it." Billy prayed she'd turn around, look at him, and tell him she changed her mind. "I love you, Billy, but I think it would be a good idea if we didn't have contact for a while."

57

Billy sat there, paralyzed. She walked out and shut the door on their lives together. He heard her car start, then pull away. He sat there. The sweat of his untouched glass of juice ran down to the table. This was happening; she didn't want Billy around. She was kicking him out to secure her false happiness. She was choosing her "man" over Billy.

Thirty minutes passed before Billy pulled himself together. He downed the orange juice, wiped away the tears he didn't realize were accumulating on his cheeks, and gathered his belongings. It didn't take long. When you don't have much, you don't have that much to pack. He filled a trash bag of the few child-hood mementos and clothes he possessed and tossed it into the back of his car.

One last time, Billy looked longingly at the house he once thought of as "home." He drove away, not knowing where he was going until he parked in front of the cliché house with its white picket fence and rich green lawn, generic red begonias lining the walkway. It was a single-story, cookie-cutter ranch house flying a Confederate flag along with the American one.

He was on autopilot. He didn't even remember texting Teddy he was coming over, that he needed to see him; it was an emergency. He tossed his beat-up phone in the passenger seat and ignored the multiple texts and calls coming from Teddy. He just had to *see* Teddy.

Billy hadn't been to Teddy's house in years, not since it became known he had a panache for dick. Not since the bloodied lips and name-calling the school turned a blind eye to. Not since everyone blamed the bullying on Billy because they said he was "flaunting himself."

He got out of his car. Billy hadn't taken the first step onto the sidewalk when the door opened and Teddy appeared. Billy's heart soared temporarily, faltering when he saw Teddy shaking his head. His heart came crashing down when Debra appeared by his side.

Billy's hand fell away from the gate latch, watching himself erased from Teddy's life with the kiss on the cheek she gave him. Billy saw it in the smug Southern, tight smile and death glare she gave him before disappearing back into the house. She had marked her territory. She knew, and probably always knew.

Billy watched the events in slow motion. Teddy shut the door behind him. He made the long trek down the thirty-foot walkway while Billy mentally pulled petals from a flower with each of his steps. Each pluck of a petal he thought, *He loves me. He loves me not.* No matter how much he willed another petal, it ended with, *He loves me not.*

"What are you doing here? This isn't a good time…" The anger in Teddy's voice hurt more than the inevitable Billy knew was about to happen.

"What is she doing here?" Billy asked with more hurt than venom.

"I said it's not a good time," Teddy repeated, not meeting Billy's eyes. "Go home, Billy."

Billy choked out, "I don't have a home anymore. My mother threw me out."

Teddy looked back at his house, then back at Billy. "I'm sorry. I wish I could help, but I'm going through my own shit right now."

"Teddy, I need you," Billy pleaded, his heart breaking. "We can just go. Leave this town, be ourselves—"

"Debra's pregnant," Teddy blurted, running his hand from his forehead to the back of his head. "Fuck, Billy. What did you think was going to happen here? That I'd say, 'fuck my future' and jump in your broken-down car and drive off like some gay country song? It's time to grow up, Billy."

Billy took a step back, and then another. He shook his head, not wanting to believe Teddy. "You never slept with her. She's a frigid bitch, right? Tell me it's not yours."

"Billy." Teddy put his hands on the gate but didn't open it. "We're getting married."

"Congratulations on the biggest mistake of your life." Billy laughed, full of hurt. As he walked to his car, Billy continued, "I hope she enjoys having her dick sucked as much as I do."

"Billy! Wait!" Teddy called out as Billy got into his car.

Billy started the engine and drove off. Two blocks later, he pulled over and cried. Yet another person in his life had proved to him their love was a lie. He wasn't sure what he was going to do. He grabbed his phone, noticing Shadow's number. His finger hovered over it.

What do I have to lose?

Joe was waiting for him on the front porch of the old two-story Southern home nestled in the woods, down back roads and away from the world. Joe came down the steps when Billy stepped out of the car. He

didn't know what to say. Last night, the man obviously didn't like him, and Billy doubted much had changed in the hours since they parted.

"I sent everyone away. I figured you could use some time to get settled before they subject you to their drama," Joe said, greeting him. Billy's lip trembled. He tried to speak, but nothing came out. Joe pulled him into a hug. Holding Billy tight, he whispered, "Let it out. It's okay to cry."

Joe kissed the top of his head. The dam holding back all of Billy's emotions burst. His legs became weak, but Joe held him. They stood there, Billy crying and asking, "Why?" Joe simply held him wishing he could answer the question. That's how they stayed until Billy shed his last tear.

"Let's get you settled. You can room with Mario. He's rarely here," Joe said, visibly holding back his own emotions.

Billy nodded, wiping his nose with the back of his arm. They grabbed his few belongings, and Billy followed Joe up the stairs to the house, then upstairs to his new bedroom. One side looked like a rainbow unicorn drag queen exploded, decorated with feather boas, rainbows, and glittery pictures. Billy's side was bare, aside from the bed with the fresh linen on it.

Billy laid his things on the bed. He turned to Joe and dropped to his knees. Trembling hands that reached for Joe's pants were caught by the wrist and used to bring Billy back up to his feet. He tried to shake Joe's grip off so he could grab his stuff and run out, but Joe wouldn't let go, no matter how hard he fought.

"This isn't about that," Joe told him, pulling Billy back into a hug. "My God, hasn't anyone ever done something nice for you without expecting something in return?" Joe's voice caught with emotion. "Billy, you can stay here as long as you want or need. No strings, do you hear me? No strings."

"Thank you," Billy said into Joe's chest, hugging the man back. "Thank you."

8

JULIA CHILD, NECROPHILIA, AND SLEEPOVERS

JORDAN WAS CONCERNED about Billy. He hadn't said anything on the drive home. When they finally pulled into a parking spot at their complex, Billy just sat there until Jordan called his name several times. He knew he didn't know Billy that well, but he could tell this wasn't normal. He could see something was wrong with him, that Billy was hurting.

When they were at Billy's door, Jordan felt he had to say something. "I really enjoyed today, thank you. You don't want to grab something to eat, do you?" Jordan asked, noticing a slight curve of a smile on Billy's face before it fell again. Jordan could tell Billy didn't want to be alone right now. "My treat?"

Billy's normal self flashed in his eyes, though his face didn't show it.

"Unless you're full from eating all that ass on camera…" Jordan teased. Billy cracked a smile. "There he is. What do you say? Let's grab something to eat?"

Billy's face lit up, and he stated, "I'll do one better. I'll make you dinner."

Jordan laughed. He hadn't encountered many people out here who could actually cook. It was all prepackaged, microwaveable, pop-in-the-oven, home meal delivery. The people he knew who *did* attempt to cook owned a fire extinguisher and had poison control on speed dial. "You can cook? Like, real food?"

Billy reached up and tweaked Jordan's nose. "Of course, you silly goose. Go get freshened up, and I'll be over in a bit." Billy opened his door. "After dinner, I can paint your nails."

"You're not painting my nails," Jordan protested. Billy waived a dismissive hand over his shoulder. "You're not painting my nails!" he repeated to Billy's closed door.

Thirty minutes later, Jordan was showered. The notifications for his Twitter were growing in number, especially after Colton took a selfie with him on set. The experience was great; he learned a lot and had a blast talking with the crew, but it hadn't inspired him to write anything like Billy hoped.

Jordan was staring at that blank screen again when Billy knocked on the door. He answered the door, narrowing his eyes at Billy who was standing in his doorway holding a bag from a restaurant down the street. "What? Don't judge me," Billy said, pushing his way in and setting the bags on the kitchen counter. Jordan shut the door and crossed his arms. "A major rule in cooking is making sure you have something defrosted, so you can cook it."

"You don't have any groceries in your apartment, do you?" Jordan accused.

"No, that's why I grabbed burgers and fries," Billy admitted. "Tomorrow we'll go grocery shopping, and I'll make you something. Promise."

Jordan joined Billy in the kitchen, their bodies uncomfortably close. "You don't have to cook me dinner. Just admit you don't know how to cook."

Billy turned around to confront Jordan, their noses nearly brushing. "I can cook. Can you?"

"I can't even boil water, but I'm man enough to admit it." Jordan swallowed hard, feeling the heat of Billy's body so close to his.

"Are you?" Jordan heard the seductive tone in Billy's voice before he quickly self-corrected. "Um, yeah. Well, I can cook, and I'm going to cook you a meal. Julia Child has nothing on me."

"I'm not eating a turducken. Just so you know, I'm haunting you if you kill me with your cooking," Jordan joked, stepping away, needing to put some distance between Billy and him.

Billy began removing the food from the bag, saying, "You're not going to die. Also, that's sweet. You want to spend your eternal afterlife with me."

"That's not what I..." Jordan began to protest before stopping himself. "You know what? Sure, why not? I want to spend my eternal afterlife with you, and while you're sleeping, I'll put my ghost dick in your mouth."

Billy pulled two plates out of Jordan's cabinet. "Hot. Also … kind of creepy. Like, would you just shove your ghost dick in my mouth, or would you nuzzle your ghost dick against my lips until I opened my mouth and just started sucking on it?"

Jordan cocked his head at Billy. "Nuzzled my ghost dick against your lips?"

Billy started plating the food for them. "Grab us something to drink. But yeah, nuzzle. You know, like rubbing it across my lips, tempting my unconscious body. Hey, would that be necrophilia?"

Jordan nearly dropped the glass at the question. "Can we, please, change the subject?"

Billy grabbed silverware out of the drawer for them, asking, "Okay, did you get inspired to write something?"

"Alright, back to the necrophilia question," Jordan pronounced, pouring them both a glass of soda to drink. "No, it would not because a ghost doesn't have a body."

"Huh." Billy took the plates to the rarely used kitchen table. "Nothing? Not even a glimmer of an idea from today?"

Jordan set their drinks down. It wasn't lost on Jordan that he had actually known Billy less than twenty-four hours, and Billy was intimately familiar with his place. "Don't get me wrong: I had a blast. I don't know… it just didn't spark anything, you know?"

Billy sat down, waiting for Jordan to sit before he began. "No, the only thing I know how to do is have sex."

Sitting down, Jordan scoffed, "Bullshit. You can act. What I saw today on that set was acting. You may not call it that, but everything that led up to the sex was acting."

Billy looked down at his plate and speared green beans with his fork. "I'm not an actor. I'm just a guy that gets paid to have sex on camera."

Jordan reached out and took Billy's hand. They both stared at it for a moment before Jordan pulled it back. "Hey, you're more than a guy who gets paid to have sex on camera."

"Thank you. You're sweet." Billy played with the food on his plate.

"I'll make you a deal," Jordan offered. Billy looked up at him, curious where this was going. "I'll call myself a writer if you call yourself an actor. Not a porn actor, but an *actual* actor."

"Write me something I'd want to perform, and you got yourself a deal," Billy countered, looking over at the abandoned tablet on the table. "I want my first non-porn debut to be written by you."

Jordan sighed. "Fine, but I don't know how to write scripts. I'm more of a short story guy."

"Guess you better learn. Just like gay porn, there's more work if you're versatile." Billy popped the green beans into his mouth, his face smug and triumphant.

After dinner, Billy poured himself a vodka cran- berry, while Jordan drank rum and ginger ale. They played Truth, No Dare; it was Billy's idea. "I want to get to know you better," he said as they settled down on the couch. "Plus, you get to know more about me. The real me."

Jordan took a sip of his cocktail. "Okay, but we can pass on a question if it makes us uncomfortable."

Billy took Jordan's free hand and examined his nails. "No passes. Jesus, your nails." Jordan yanked his hand back. "You're getting a manicure."

Jordan looked at the insistent look on Billy's face. "Fine. A manicure, but you're not painting my nails."

"We'll see. You go first." Billy grinned, sitting back on the couch and sipping his drink.

Jordan thought for a moment and chose his first question, "Okay, have you ever been in love with someone?"

Billy shifted uncomfortably, thinking about his answer. "Right for the jugular, huh? No. I thought I loved him, but looking back, he taught me what love isn't." The ice in Billy's glass rattled as he downed most of his drink. "What about you? Have you ever been in love?"

"I thought I was," Jordan said easily, taking a swig of his drink. "I was dating this guy for three years. I was about to ask him to move in with me. All my friends hated him because he would make these needling comments about me and my weight."

Jordan looked into his glass, not wanting to see the pity in Billy's eyes. "His pet name for me was Shamu. Whenever we went out to eat, he'd order me salad with no dressing, telling me I didn't need the calories." Jordan rolled the drink in his glass. "When I started jogging, he'd say California didn't need any more earthquakes."

Billy reached out and took Jordan's free hand. "Wow. He sounds like a real jerk."

Jordan shrugged. "He also told me my writing was shit. I really haven't been able to write since then. Not like I used to." Jordan raised his gaze. There was a light in his eyes. "I used to write constantly about everything."

Billy patted his hand. "We'll get you back there, and if you need anything, I'm here. Gym buddy? I'm there. Come over in the middle of the night and eat ice cream right out of the carton? Fuck yeah, I'm there." Billy squeezed Jordan's hand and added, "You know you're perfect the way you are... right?"

"Knowing it and believing it are two different things," said Jordan.

Billy's phone chimed, and he let go of Jordan's hand. Pulling out his phone, Billy began frantically typing.

"Oh, no... you're not tweeting that are you?" Jordan asked.

Billy gave Jordan an incredulous look. "No. Walter texted me asking if you'd be interested in being the meat in a bear sandwich tomorrow. The guy they scheduled backed out at the last minute." Billy studied Jordan. "See? He thinks you're hot enough for porn. Are you interested?"

Jordan answered emphatically, "No. If there's one thing I learned today, it's that it's hard work doing porn."

Billy scrunched his face in thought. "It is; I never thought about it. I'll tell him you said no." Billy sent the message. "Okay, your turn."

Jordan took Billy's empty glass to refresh their drinks. He asked, "What's the hardest part of doing porn? And don't say the dicks."

Billy laughed, turning to watch Jordan. "Fuck you. I would say it's the fans. They think because you do porn, they can touch you inappropriately, and it's okay because you do porn. Oh, thank you." Billy took his drink from Jordan when he returned, both glasses full. They clinked glasses and both took a sip.

"Or," Billy continued, "they think they have a right to dictate what you do. When I grew out my hair, this guy slid into my DM's telling me I needed to cut my hair because I looked feminine." Billy groaned. "When I told him I liked my hair long, he told me I didn't know what I was doing. I politely told him to fuck off. Then, he called me a diva."

Jordan shook his head. "People can be asses. I'm sorry you have to go through that. Do you need me to be your bodyguard?"

Billy's smile faltered, remembering all the beatings he took in high school and how they stopped when Billy laid the captain of the football team on his ass in the middle of the school's courtyard. He'd been suspended for a week, but no one dared pick a fight with him after that incident. "No. This diva has nice nails she ain't afraid to break."

Billy sat his glass down. He rubbed his hands together in anticipation, stating, "My turn! Why won't you let me paint your nails?"

Jordan groaned, rolling his eyes, "Billy, I won't let you paint my nails because…" Jordan thought for a moment. "You know what? What the hell? Paint my nails."

Billy jumped up in triumph. "Yes! I'll be right back. I just need to get my stuff. This teacher-dude came out with a whole line of male nail polish. You'll love it."

Jordan laughed at Billy rushing out of his place. Something nagged at him, though ... what Billy said about his fans. Anyone who meets Billy knew he wasn't a diva. He was a sweetheart and more than just a sexy body to watch and get off to. Billy was a person, not a commodity.

Lying in bed that night, his nails painted a deep, rich purple, Jordan couldn't get that absurd thought of his head. Billy slept next to him, curled up like a baby. He had sheepishly asked if he could spend the night, using the excuse he was too drunk to drive home. Jordan hadn't argued, only laughed and told him to brush his teeth.

Slipping out of bed and careful not to disturb Billy, Jordan headed to the living room where his nemesis rested. He turned on the tablet and connected his Bluetooth keyboard. He loaded up his document program. The evil blinking cursor appeared.

"Fuck you. Buckle your seat belt. You're going for a ride," Jordan said softly.

Jordan awoke on the couch the next morning with his feet resting in Billy's lap. He was still half-asleep, observing Billy sip his coffee and read from the tablet. He was about to lay his head back down when he realized what Billy was reading.

Jordan shot up and tried to snatch the tablet from Billy. "Don't read that! It's not done!"

Billy twisted to keep Jordan from taking the tablet, careful not to spill his coffee. "I'm not done! This is good. Like, really good. It's funny, makes a statement and…" He looked at Jordan. "I want to make it."

Jordan stopped mid-lunge, asking, "Really? You're not just saying that? You really like it?"

"Yeah. When you're done, can we make it?" Billy asked, settling down.

"How?" Jordan asked, wiping the sleep from his eyes. "We'd need sets, actors, camera men, sound people … and more importantly, money to *pay* those people."

Jordan didn't know what to make of the devious smile Billy flashed at him. "You leave that to me. You just finish *this*," Billy said, sliding the tablet onto the table. "Coffee?"

9

WITHOUT YOU

MARIO RUBBED THE lotion into his long, smooth, almond-brown legs. He couldn't believe he was still doing this, not that there were many men willing to pay for his services anymore. They wanted the ultra-masculine generic white boy, and Mario couldn't give them that because he wasn't white or generic.

Standing up, he looked at himself in the dirty floor-length mirror. *I still look good.* He adjusting the red G-string covering his naughty bits. His hand ran over the scar that ran up his left thigh.

He could hide it with makeup, but it felt wrong to do so. That scar was from the night his life veered off course, instead of heading into his dream future. The scar served as a reminder of who he was, who he could have been, and who he was now. If the men he entertained didn't like it, they could just fuck off.

Mario slipped on the matching red teddy. The man coming tonight wanted the same fantasy so many other men who darkened his doorstep wanted. They thought because he was half Asian, he was one of those lady-boys they heard about, but nothing could be further from the truth. Cross his palm with cash, though, and he could play nearly any fantasy.

He got through the early years of his life by pretending. He pretended to be straight for his Marine father who tried to "toughen him up" with sports and shooting guns. He pretended to be naive and innocent for those men he allowed to seduce him in the bars. The only time he didn't pretend was with Randy.

With Randy he never had to pretend. Sure, he painted his face and slipped into women's clothing when they went out on the town, but that was to keep the men whose necks were redder than the Devil's dick from starting trouble. Men who catcalled and whistled at him as they undressed his petite slender body with their eyes. He wondered when they got to his eight-inch tucked dick, did they look at it with disgust or delight?

Randy always looked at it with delight, ever since the first moment between them. He remembered, however, that at first Randy scared the shit out of him. When Randy first opened the door to his little one-bedroom apartment, Mario nearly ran. He was certain it was a trick, that Randy had lured him there, and once inside, Mario would get his ass beat.

Standing in front of Mario was a man who looked like a real cowboy calendar pin-up. He was a six-foot tall, clean shaven, squared-jaw country boy. He was wearing a button-down dress shirt—sleeves rolled up—faded denim jeans that hugged his body, a belt buckle comically too big, and the stereotypical cowboy hat.

Then, he did the unexpected, and Mario knew he'd be with this man forever. He took his hat off, revealing his short chestnut brown hair, placed it over his heart, and declared in his deep country draw, "My God, you're beautiful."

Mario didn't go home that night. The only reason he went home to Joe's the next morning was because he had to film with Brett and had a paid date that night. It was with one of those Southern want-to-be-aristocratic-social-elite types. The ones who paid him for a date ... and his silence.

This clientele wanted Mario for the illusion of being heterosexual when they went out with "Maria," not Mario, draped on their arm for the gossip mongers. These men would continue living their lie later that night when "Maria" roughly fucked them raw in their beds because it wasn't gay if they swallowed the evidence.

But Randy didn't need the illusion; he accepted Mario for who he was: a five-foot confident, timid, sexy, Filipino man with a big heart and an even bigger dick. He didn't even care that Mario escorted or filmed porn; just like Mario, he saw it as a means to an end. A paycheck. Because Mario always came home to Randy.

That was two years before Mario met Billy. By then, Randy and Mario were a year deep into their dream: living in an old house they purchased set on an acre of tree-covered land, while Randy cleared the trees and built their new, real home.

But this dream came crashing to an end a few months after Billy left the Country Boyz, and Mario woke up in a hospital bed, body aching, pain in his leg, and Randy no place to be seen. The crash haunted Mario every day since then.

He remembered that night... Driving home with Randy from the bar down the dark back roads, he was laughing with Randy, singing along to a painfully sad country song. The lights of the other vehicle just popped to life out of nowhere, and whether Randy swerved left or right, the lights followed, intent on hunting them.

He remembered screaming as Randy veered off the road to avoid the oncoming vehicle, slamming them into a tree. Then, it all went black. He remembered hearing a young, callous, male voice, off in the distance that said, "Oh, wow. This chick's got a dick." Mario wanted to slap the owner of that mouth but drifted out of consciousness again.

He awoke—days later—in a cold, sterile, hospital room. His body ached, his thigh throbbed with pain, and the only thing he wanted to do was see Randy. The hospital staff finally told him after hours of screaming and threatening that Randy hadn't made it. Mario went numb after that, and then he cried and didn't stop... not even when he was dragged out of the hospital by Joe and Brett.

Soon after, however, he did stop. Stopped crying. Stopped talking. Stopped eating. Stopped showering. Stopped the will to live. Without Randy, there was no point. They had a life together, dreams together. Without Randy, there was no life or dream for Mario.

Brett and Joe nursed him the best they could, changing his bandage, forcing him to eat and bathe. He fought with them, spit on them, begged them to just let him die, but they wouldn't. They let him hurt. They helped him heal and work through his pain.

It was hard at first, when Mario eventually came home to the broken dreams, the memories of Randy. He had quit the website and the escorting. He was too ashamed of the long scar on his leg. Not to mention, gossip traveled faster than the speed of light out in the country, and everyone now knew "Maria" was really Mario.

Day by day, he trudged on. Some days were better than others. Some were so soul crushing he didn't want to get out of bed, but he did. He avoided people whenever possible, even Brett and Joe. He paid his bills, his taxes, bought what he needed ... and watched his bank account dwindle.

When he had no other choice but to go back to the life he knew, the website had folded. Brett was gone. Joe was going through his own shit, Keith and Kevin were off at school, Billy was living his best life, and Shadow was rebuilding his life somewhere. Still, there were a few local Johns willing to cross his palm with bills for the exotic fantasy.

His clientele was mainly travelers too weary to drive any further on the desolate stretch of interstate, but not too tired to find a piece of ass on their apps. The man coming to visit him tonight was one of those men, hoping to sow some "wild oats" and make a memory they'd jack off to until they were sixty.

Straightening his shake-and-go pussycat wig and touching up his cheap makeup, Mario transformed himself into Maria. He practiced his walk, scooping up the bills that threatened final notice, notice of foreclosure, and the like. He tossed them into a drawer. Those were a Mario problem. Tonight he was Maria.

Mario slipped on the matching sheer robe which left nothing to the imagination. The look was almost complete; all he needed were the come-fuck-me pumps he hadn't been able to wear since the accident. Not since that piece of metal cut both flesh and muscle nearly to the bone and severed nerves that didn't quite work right once they healed.

The rap on his door took him out of his spin into self-misery. Men didn't pay him to cry. "Coming!" Mario called in the demure feminine voice he used for Maria.

He took a moment to seal the persona before he opened the door. "Hello," he said in his most sultry voice to the looming faceless figure dressed in all black. "Oh, honey, you don't need all that. My nearest neighbor is three miles down the road."

The figure said nothing, but stepped forward, causing Mario to stumble back. "Cash up front," Mario blurted out, trying to keep the fear out of his voice. "No cash, no ass."

The imposing figure did not speak or move. Mario decided he'd had enough. "Okay, you can get the fuck out right—"

Mario's injured leg faltered with the backhanded slap across his cheek. He stumbled and fell, his head nearly catching the edge of the coffee table. Seething,

he began to lift himself, growling in his deep Mario voice, "Oh, you've done fucked up, asshole."

Before Mario could make good on his threat, a gloved hand gripped Mario by the head. The hand did what the fall did not and slammed Mario's head into the coffee table. Stars exploded in Mario's vision. "Mother," Mario slurred before his head connected with the table again and again, until there was a pop in his head and his body went limp.

The edges of Mario's vision began to darken. He felt his sagging arms being lifted. Something was being wrapped around his wrists and then his ankles. He saw the shadowy man standing over him in the glint of metal of an old Zippo lighter. There was a flicker of flame dancing out the top.

"Burn in Hell," the emotionless male voice said, tossing the lighter onto the couch. "Freak."

As he heard the crackle of fire, Mario watched the booted feet leave. The darkness expanded in his vision. *Finally, I'll be with you again, my love.* Mario held on to the image of Randy smiling at him in his mind. *For all eternity.*

The darkness took hold as the flames grew, burning away the final remains of the dream Mario and Randy once had.

DO YOU SEE WHAT I SEE?

"**G**o! I **CAN'T** write with you hovering! I'll come get you when I'm done!" Jordan yelled finally, pointing to the door.

Billy didn't take offense to Jordan kicking him out of the apartment. He knew he was hovering over Jordan while he tried to write. He read over Jordan's shoulder, sitting beside him and leaning into the screen. He was surprised it took Jordan two hours to actually kick him out. He would have done it after fifteen minutes.

Billy decided to be productive. Instead of sitting around his apartment among the unpacked boxes and hastily purchased furniture, he resolved to shop for groceries. He didn't have much in his cupboards, and from his time at Jordan's, he knew he could use a few things. He'd get them food and make Jordan that home-cooked meal he promised.

Disguising himself with a ball cap, Billy headed off to the local supermarket. It wasn't likely he'd be recognized, but it was better safe than sorry. He didn't want to be checking out cucumbers and someone ask if he was going to use that in one of his videos. He regretted having made that cliché video.

Pushing his cart through the produce, Billy pulled out his phone. He hadn't checked in with Carlos in about a week. Carlos was his lifeline to whom Billy considered his East coast family, and Billy wished he could be there for all of them after what happened to Dennis. Though they said it was fine, Billy still felt like shit for not being there.

"Hey, slut. How's the Wild West?" Carlos's cheery voice answered through the phone.

"Hey, bitch. How's the gang doing?" Billy laughed, picking up a tomato and pretending to examine it.

"As well as can be expected. It's really fucked up, you know?" Carlos said, his cheery disposition disappearing.

Billy tossed the tomato into a plastic bag, sighing, "I wish I could have been there for you. I wish I could be there for Dennis."

Carlos cut him off before he could blame himself any further. "You were on a plane when it happened, and you have your obligations there."

"Yeah, but—"

Carlos interrupted him, "No 'buts,' except the ones we fuck. Speaking of butts we fuck, are you and that writer you posted about making the neighbors complain about the noise?"

Billy moved on from tomatoes, picking up a cucumber and smiling at his salacious thought.

"No. That's how we met, though. I was making too much noise."

"Practicing or rehearsing?" Carlos asked, hoping for the former, but expecting the latter.

Billy sighed, adding the cucumber to his cart and moving on to the lettuce. "Rehearsing. I was bored. I don't have any friends out here like you guys."

"Have you tried? I know you know a lot of people out there," Carlos accused.

A head of lettuce joined the tomato and cucumber in Billy's cart. "I do. I normally want to go out and party, but I just don't really want to now, you know?"

"How are you supposed to show me all the hot bars and even hotter men if you don't go out and find them? Promise me you'll go out this weekend," Carlos ordered with a detectable smile through the phone.

Billy moved down the meat aisle and surrendered, "Fine. I promise I'll see if Jordan wants to go out."

"Uh, huh, and how long have you known this Jordan?" Carlos asked suspiciously.

Billy tossed two steak packages into the cart. "I met him Friday. Ugh, I forgot the baked potatoes."

"Uh, huh... what are you doing right now?" Carlos asked.

Billy turned his cart around. "Grocery shopping for our dinner. I want to show him I can actually cook."

"Okay..." Carlos drawled. "Have you ... slept with him?"

Billy stopped, shocked. "What? No. I only cuddled with him in bed the last two nights." Billy glared at a nosey woman nearby who made a disapproving noise. Billy stuck his tongue out at her retreating back. "We're just friends."

"What else are you picking up at the store?"

"I need to get us some more popcorn, some juice… oh, I need to get some tea so I can make him some real Southern sweet tea. I'm going to get us some healthy snacks and a few sweet treats," Billy said excitedly into the phone.

"Billy, do you hear yourself?" Carlos asked.

Billy shrugged, moving his cart through the market. "What? I just told you my list."

Carlos's tone was serious. "You have your own place, but you said you're shopping for the two of you. You officially met the guy two days nights ago and you've spent two nights in his bed, and I'm betting you're planning on spending the night again tonight."

Billy didn't want to admit it what Carlos was implying. "What are you saying?"

Carlos spoke with a smile in his voice. "You like him, Billy. You're might not want to admit it, but you like him."

Billy navigated through the market, stopping to look at things on the shelves. He mentally debated on whether to toss the various items into the cart or move on. "Of course I like him. He's my new best friend out here."

Carlos didn't argue. "Okay, so you won't admit it yet. I get it. Let me know when you do."

"Anyways, Carlos," Billy changed the subject as he turned the corner and nearly slammed into the nosy woman from the produce aisle. She shot him a death glare again. He stuck his tongue out at her for good measure and moved on. "He's writing this script, and I was wondering if you could ask Dennis if he'd read it. You know, give him some notes on it. Editing pointers."

"I'll ask him, but why don't you?"

"You'll know the right time to ask. With all he went through and is still going through..." Billy sighed. "Also, in case he's mad at me."

Carlos reaffirmed, "He's not mad at you. None of us are. I'll have him contact you, okay?"

Billy stopped in front of the ice cream and grabbed the chocolate and vanilla oat milk dairy alternatives. "Thanks, Carlos. You're a good friend."

Billy could feel the love in Carlos's voice. "You are, too, Billy. But I'll be pissed if you break that boy's heart."

"I don't like him like that," Billy groaned. "Alright, I got to go check out. Love you, mean it."

"Love you, mean it."

Billy ended the call and looked at the cart full of groceries. He thought about what Carlos said. *I don't like Jordan like that.* Billy moved toward the check out. *Jordan is just a good friend. I just don't see what Carlos is seeing.* Billy started scanning his items. *I just don't see it.*

MINE IS BIGGER

BRETT SAT AT the table in the cold interrogation room. His body still shook from what he saw when he walked through Joe's door that morning. He stared blankly at the officers while they kept asking him the same questions over and over again. He answered their questions in a flat, monotone voice. His answers never changed, no matter how they twisted their questions, talked sweetly to him, yelled, or threatened him.

Brett kept reliving that moment in his mind … standing there, looking at Joe's crumbled, bloated body at the bottom of the stairs. Flies swarmed around the body, attracted to the smell of its decaying flesh. The stench filled Brett's nostrils and his stomach churned. Then, he was running out the front door into the yard, stopping only to empty the contents of his stomach.

"Holy fuck!" Brett cried out, wiping his mouth with the back of his hand. "Holy fuck, fuck, fuck!"

He pulled out his phone and called 9-1-1. The moment the operator answered, he began blurting out words. "Bottom of stairs. Dead. My friend. Help. Please." Brett took in a deep breath, trying to organize his muddled mind. He started again, "My friend. I found him dead at the bottom of the stairs."

Brett was in the yard pacing aimlessly, smoking cigarette after cigarette and chanting, "No, no, no, no," when the police cruiser arrived. A uniformed officer cautiously put his arm around Brett and guided him to sit down on a bench while the others went inside. Soon, the entire front yard was filled with police cruisers and paramedics, faceless people asking him questions.

"Are you okay?"

"How did you know the deceased?"

"Do you know what happened?"

"Is there someone we can call?"

"When was the last time you saw him alive?"

Brett looked at them with haunted eyes. He remembered the last time he saw Joe. Billy had been gone almost a year, snapped up by the major studio circuit. Shadow left a note saying he needed a life without porn. Mario wasn't talking to either of them after losing Randy. Kevin and Keith had stopped coming around to film… and it was just Joe and him in that big house.

Fan content sites had started emerging on the social media platforms. They were steadily eating away from the Country Boyz subscriptions. They were cheaper, had more videos, posted more often, and interacted with their subscribers. Joe and Brett couldn't keep up with the competition; they could only post so many videos of Brett jacking off. Joe finally decided to pull the plug and shut down the site.

The day after they shut down the site, Brett looked at Joe with remorse in his heart and eyes. "It was a good run," he had said, shaking Joe's hand. They both knew without saying a word they would be parting ways. The porn site was the only thing keeping Brett there. It was the only reason Joe tolerated Brett's reckless behavior.

Brett went upstairs, grabbed the bags he had packed, and silently left. He tossed the bags into the backseat of the beat-up car he never got around to fixing up. Starting the car and pulling into the dirt road that led toward the highway, Brett expected to see Joe in his rearview mirror. Joe wasn't there.

He pulled onto the highway, heading north for no other reason than he thought that's where Shadow would have gone. He drove until both the gas gauge and his stomach were riding on empty. He could only afford to fill up one of them; most of his money over the last year was spent like running water flowed as they expected the failing site to suddenly become profitable.

Brett paid the cashier—a man a few years older than him, in grease-stained coveralls and mousy, brown hair which hung in ringlets around his kind eyes. When Brett asked for the bathroom, the man's thin lips spread into a smile. He either recognized Brett from his videos or just figured the broken man was easy prey.

"Bathroom is in the back. The lock's broken." The man casually grabbed his crotch.

Brett eyed the scruffy-faced man. He found the man attractive in that rough-around-the-edges way. "Is that so? So, anyone could just walk in?"

"I could just lock the front door, close up the register, and…" the man ran his tongue over the top of his lip, "stand guard for you."

Brett stepped back and cupped his own crotch blatantly. "Or you could lock the front door, pull fifty from the register, and after I'm finished pissing, you hand me that fifty and suck my dick."

"Counteroffer," the man retorted, turning some keys in the register and locking it. "You go back there, take your piss. I'll lock that front door and then make those pretty eyes of yours roll back in your head when I shove my cock up that cute little ass of yours."

"I don't bottom. I only top," Brett said fervently.

The man winked at Brett, "I'm verse. I've seen how you handle those young boys in your video. I think it's time a real man showed you how it's really done."

Brett laughed. "You think you're going to top me? If you've seen my videos, you should know that isn't going to happen."

The man put his hands on the counter. "I'll make you a deal. Biggest dick tops."

Brent crossed his arms. "I don't top for free. Fifty dollars."

The man winked at Brett. "Confident that you got the bigger dick, huh? Go on, take a piss. I'll be back there in a minute."

"Don't forget to bring the cash," Brett replied and walked toward the back of the store. Stepping into the tiny one-toilet bathroom, Brett laughed. In all his years, only Billy came close to his size. He pulled out his cock, shot a hot stream from his bladder, and laughed aloud, "I can't believe he thinks his cock is bigger than mine."

"Oh, I know it is. Are you done yet? I'd like to collect my prize." Brett turned his head to see the man leaning against the open door.

Brett turned from the toilet, stroking his cock. "You mean *my* prize. If you want to save yourself the embarrassment, you can just hand me my money, then drop to your knees and suck it."

The man pushed off the door frame with his shoulder. He unzipped his coveralls and let them fall to the floor. "Your dick is big. Mine is definitely bigger." He stepped out of his clothes. The man had a slight belly, and his skin was pasty-white except for his farmer's tan.

"Jesus. You're not putting that in me," Brett declared, staring at the dangling meat between his legs that almost reached his knees, and it wasn't even fully hard.

The man crossed the bathroom and slipped an arm around Brett's waist, hand going down the back of his pants. "I'll have you begging for me to slide it in."

Brett opened his mouth to protest but found the man's mouth on his, whiskers scratching his face. The hand on Brett's ass pulled him hard against the stranger. Brett's first instinct was to push the man away, punch him, and run. The second was to let him have his way and live in the moment.

Brett weakly hit the man in the chest with his fist. The next pound was barely a tap. Then he unfurled his fist and grabbed the stranger by the back of the head, pulling him into a hard kiss. Slipping his other arm around the stranger's waist, Brett rubbed their cocks together.

Brett kicked off his shoes, then his pants. They broke the kiss only long enough for the stranger to yank Brett's shirt off, then they were back on each other like animals, kissing roughly, bodies pressed closed, arms a-tangle as they groped one another.

Lips shiny from their kiss, the man said, "Fuck. You're hotter in person."

"Shut up and fuck me like the whore I am," Brett growled, lunging at the man. Brett's lips scraped over the man's stubble, the sensation straddling the line between pleasure and pain.

Brett kissed his way down the man's neck, tasting the remnants of a hard day's work, down to the man's left nipple. Brett ran his tongue over the nub before grazing his teeth over it.

The man groaned, holding Brett's head against his chest, "That's it, boy. Chew Daddy's nipple."

Brett did, careful not to chew too hard. Being called "boy" had a cathartic effect on him. It just clicked. Brett was doing this for pure pleasure. There were no cameras to worry about, no angles he was trying to get. More importantly, it wasn't about the money shot. It was about the journey to it.

Brett moved down the man's body, adorning the slightly soft and furry belly with kisses as he dropped to his knees. It was there, right in front of him: this random stranger's cock, thick, hard, lined with veins that ended with a flared head and a pearl of pre-cum glistening on its tip.

Confronted with the behemoth cock, Brett reached out and took it in his hand. He was barely able to get his hand around it. Wide-eyed, Brett stroked the cock, dislodging the pearl, sending it cascading to the ground with a sticky trail. It was huge and intimidating.

"Go on. It won't bite, but I might," the man teased.

Brett inhaled deeply, steeling his nerves. With trepidation, Brett aimed the cock at his open mouth and stretched his whisker-raw lips around it. He swallowed what he could of the gargantuan cock into his mouth, the rest he worked with his hands.

"That's it, baby. Nurse off Daddy's cock," the man said with a delighted sigh.

Brett gurgled a moan as the man stroked his hand over his nearly shaved head. He couldn't get all of the man down, his cock almost as impossibly thick as it was long. He took what he could, barely tasting the steady stream of pre-cum trickling down his throat.

Brett had a moment of nostalgia. The days before he was worried about content, to the days when the ache in his jaw wasn't something to push through until someone ended the shot. The days when he was red-eyed, nose running, mouth sparkling from spit and pre-cum. The times when it was about the actual sex and not how they could sell it.

The stranger groaned, one hand still petting Brett's head, the other playing with his nipple. "Damn, that mouth feels better than I imagined. I can't wait to sink into that tight little ass."

If it weren't for the monstrous cock filling his mouth, restricting his breath and trapping his tongue, Brett would have halfheartedly protested. The protest would have only been for show; before he and Shadow began filming, they had flip-fucked, and he enjoyed it, but the fans preferred it when he topped.

"Okay, man," the man said and pulled his cock from Brett's aching jaw. "Let me get a taste of you."

"Damn, your cock is big," Brett gasped, allowing himself to be pulled up to his feet.

"And I know how to fit it in tight places." The man grabbed Brett by the back of the head and pulled him into a kiss. He dropped down to his knees in front of Brett. "Nice fucking cock," he said, stroking Brett's cock. "Woof."

"Oh, God! Jesus!" Brett cried out when his cock was swallowed whole. Brett spread his legs to keep from buckling under the pleasure of his cock buried in a warm throat. "You'd make a killing in porn with a cock and mouth like that."

The man pulled off Brett's cock and stroked it while he looked up at Brett. "My husband says the same thing."

Before Brett could say anything, the man reached around and took a cheek in each hand and furiously began fucking his mouth with Brett's cock. Brett steadied himself with a hand on the man's shoulder. "Damn, that mouth. Man, I haven't been blown in ages."

The man pulled off and asked, "Who is crazy enough to pass up this cock?" Without waiting for an answer, he sucked Brett back down to the base. His hands were spreading Brett's cheeks apart. He slipped a finger between and stroke the nearly-virgin hole.

Brett could feel it. His balls were drawing up. His cock throbbed in the man's mouth. He was going to blow his load right down this stranger's throat. He fought the instinct to pull out and beat off onto the man's face. Instead Brett squeezed his shoulder and moaned, "You're going to make me cum."

The man pulled off Brett's cock and spun him around. "Not till I get my prize. I'm going to fuck this ass."

Brett let out a slight yelp of surprise at the hard press of the man's tongue licking at his hole. Spreading his legs farther, he arched his back. Brett grabbed his cheeks and pulled them farther apart. Brett moaned, enjoying the rough feel of scruff and tender touch of tongue. "Fuck yeah, rim my hole."

"Tasty hole. I'm going to destroy this ass," the man mumbled into Brett's ass.

"Destroy it. Fucking destroy it!" Brett found himself begging.

"Your wish is my command. I'll go slow." Brett felt a hard slap on his ass and the man's hand on his hips as he stood. The man put a hand on Brett's back and bent him over the sink. "Let me know if I hurt you."

Holding onto the sink and looking into the mirror at the stranger, Brett inhaled deeply and let it out. He wished he had poppers or something stronger. "Lube. It's been awhile."

The man disappeared from behind Brett. Brett turned his head to watch the man's tight furry ass as he went to his overhauls and pulled out a green bottle. "Of course. Almond oil. I hope you're not allergic to nuts."

Brett closed his eyes and took another deep soothing breath. "Funny. I don't know if I can take all of you."

He drizzled the lube down Brett's crack. Brett felt a finger pressed into him. "You *are* tight." Brett took another deep breath with the stretch of a second finger, then another breath with the third finger, and finally a fourth. "Tight, but loose. I like that. Just tell me when."

"Just put it in me already. Get it over with," Brett growled.

The fingers left. Brett felt the fat head of the man's cock pressing into him. "Relax, baby. You can do it." Brett took a moment to close his eyes and center himself. He pushed back, feeling the pain of the stretch with head popping in. A soothing hand ran over the small of Brett's back. "Nice and slow. You can do it."

Brett was grateful the man let him set the pace. It seemed like hours before the pain in his ass subsided and he could push back a little more. He gritted his teeth, taking a few more centering breaths. He pushed back some more, then a little more, feeling his body accept the huge dick.

"That's it. No more," Brett said, breathing heavily.

The man patted Brett's hip. "Halfway. More than most can handle their first time."

Brett watched himself in the mirror getting fucked. His face was flushed, his mind clouded with desire. The man behind him held onto his hips and guided him back and forth, the cock sliding in and out of Brett easier and easier. Brett could feel the cock sliding slightly further and further into him as the man occasionally dribbled more almond oil on his cock.

"Harder. Faster," Brett snarled.

Careful not to push too much into Brett, the man began thrusting hard. He kept a firm grip on Brett, making sure he didn't hurt him. Brett saw the pleasure and enjoyment in his own face as he took the man's dick. He spit in his hand then started stroking his own cock, careful not to bust.

The man behind Brett was panting, "Damn, boy. I'm going to breed your porn-ass."

The man behind Brett let out a grunt. Brett blew his own load, spilling his seed onto the tile of the bathroom floor. Brett arched up and back, howling as his own orgasm shuddered through his body. A hand wrapped around Brett's waist. Brett turned his head and found himself kissing the stranger again.

"Where ya heading to?" the man asked, pulling his softening cock out of Brett.

"North," Brett answered ambiguously.

The man grabbed some toilet paper and began wiping off his dick. "Cool. Don't suppose I could talk you into staying the night? My husband would love to meet you. Fuck you, too, probably."

"I don't have a place to stay around here. You offering?" Brett grabbed some toilet paper and wiped away the leaking cum.

The man pulled Brett into another kiss. "Sure. Why not? Like I said, my husband would love to fuck you too. The name is Chris."

"I'm Brett." Brett put his arms around Chris, enjoying that sense of being with someone again.

Brett never left after that night. Chris hired him to work in his shop, and the three enjoyed many evenings together with and without their clothes. Shadow became a memory, slowly and quietly fading away. Then, when Brett met Sean, he remembered happiness. It wasn't a traditional relationship, but it was theirs, and it worked for them.

"Brett, they said I can take you home." Brett looked up at Chris's concerned face, snapping out of his own thoughts.

Brett nodded. He stood, still in a daze. He let Chris guide him out of the interrogation room, then out of the station. Something just didn't sit right with him about this. Chris walked with his arm around Brett to the car, gently guided him into the seat, and fastened his seatbelt. Brett stared out the window.

"They're dead. They're really dead," Brett said to himself as he watched Chris go around to the driver's side.

12

THE SWEETEST OF DREAMS

JORDAN SPENT HIS quiet time alone finishing and polishing the script. The quiet was nice, but bothersome. The apartment seemed so empty without Billy. Even when Billy was being quiet, he seemed to fill the room with personality. Billy had been in his life less than forty-eight hours, and now Jordan couldn't imagine not having him around.

He brightened, but then scowled as Billy returned. "What is all this?" he asked when he saw Billy holding bags of groceries.

"Groceries," Billy said as if it was plain as day. He pushed past Jordan and set the bags on the kitchen counter. "Help me get the rest."

"The rest? I thought you were going to the gym?!" Jordan just stared at Billy.

Billy took Jordan by the hand and pulled him out the door. "I went shopping instead. We were running low on stuff, and I promised you a home-cooked meal."

After three trips and counters covered in bags, Jordan asked, "Isn't some of this yours?"

"Yeah, why do you ask?" Billy answered, putting things away.

"Because you're putting everything in my kitchen. Shouldn't we be putting some in your place?" Jordan began unpacking the bags.

Billy paused while putting away cereal. "No, unless you're tired of me already?"

Jordan didn't know why he did it. He went up behind Billy and put his arms around Billy, hugging him from behind. "I like having you here."

Billy patted Jordan's hands with his and answered, "Good. I like hanging with you. Oh, just so you know, we're going out Friday night."

Jordan rested his head on Billy's shoulder. "I haven't been clubbing in ages. I don't know where to go anymore."

Billy relaxed back into Jordan, enjoying the feel of being held, reassuring him, "I'll take care of that. Did you finish the script?"

Jordan gave Billy a slight squeeze. "I think so. I need to polish it up a bit."

Billy patted Jordan's hands. "Well, get to polishing. You can read it to me while I cook."

"Okay, how much do I owe you for the groceries?" Jordan gave one final squeeze before slowly pulling away.

"You'll get it next time. Now get to work. I want to hear the whole thing," Billy dismissed Jordan, returning to the groceries.

Jordan returned to his work, sitting across the couch with his back against the armrest, so he could covertly watch Billy. He read, then reread a section. He envisioned it all in his mind, changing a line here, adding another there, and changing an action there until it was perfect. Then, he did it over and over again.

When it was done, Jordan read it out loud while Billy was busy cooking. Billy would stop him every now and then, telling him to put more emotion in the words, to feel it. He did, adjusting the lines again as he read out loud. This was the first time in a long time that he wrote something he felt passionate about.

After dinner, Jordan conceded that Billy *could* actually cook. Then Billy made him admit that he *could* actually write. After that, Jordan was banished to do the dishes while Billy went on one of his rare trips to his own apartment to shower and change clothes. Jordan didn't even think twice when he handed Billy his spare key, so he could let himself back in.

After they were both refreshed, they sat on the couch watching bad television. Well, Jordan was sitting on the couch. Billy was laying across it with his head in Jordan's lap. Jordan was running his fingers through Billy's silky blonde hair. It would have been a casual, intimate moment if they were more than friends.

"What are you going to do while I'm working tomorrow?" Jordan asked, twirling Billy's hair through his fingers.

Billy huffed, "Damn, I forgot you work. I have a scene to film tomorrow. Can you take off?"

Jordan continued to play in Billy's hair, wishing he could go with Billy. "No. What are you filming tomorrow? Do you need me to go over lines with you?"

Billy sighed. "No lines. It's a bathroom glory-hole scene." Billy shifted to get this phone when he got a text notification. The grin on his face reached from one ear to the other as he read the message. "Don't be mad."

"What did you do?" Jordan narrowed his eyes at him.

Billy set the phone down and rolled over, so he was looking up at Jordan. "My friend Dennis writes the scripts for the movies he films. He's the one that does those taboo porn videos. He was the one in the news recently about that stalker that was killing homeless kids."

Jordan lightly tapped him on the forehead. "Billy, what did you do?"

Billy answered nervously. "He agreed to read what you wrote. He said he'd give you formatting tips and critique it for you."

Jordan thought about being angry, but he couldn't be. "Thank you." He tapped Billy's forehead again. "Next time, ask me first."

"I find it easier to ask for forgiveness. Send it to him when you're ready. It's really good." Yawning, Billy sat up and stretched his body. "I don't know about you, but I'm ready for bed."

In turn, Jordan yawned, "Asshole. You know yawning is contagious."

Billy stood and wiggled his butt at Jordan. "Next time I'm bad, you can spank me. You clean up in here. I'll get the bed ready."

"Promises, promises. Don't be hogging the sheet tonight!" he called out as Billy disappeared into the bedroom.

He turned the television off, put away the dishes, and finally locked up and turned off the lights. Billy was in his form-fitting green briefs fluffing up the pillows. When he turned and smiled, Jordan's heart caught for a moment, and he wondered what he was doing. Why was he torturing himself like this?

He went to climb in the bed, but Billy stopped him. Billy grabbed the bottom of Jordan's shirt. "You can't tell me you normally sleep in a shirt and shorts. I let you get away with it the last two nights, but not anymore."

Jordan's shirt came up and off. "I'm not comfortable with other people seeing my body." Jordan put his arms around his chest, trying to hide his body. "You're so perfect, and I'm so … so me."

Billy took Jordan's hands away from his chest. "You're perfect the way you are. Walter wanted you for a porn, remember?"

"Bear porn," Jordan groaned.

"He thought people would like to see you naked on camera." Billy took hold of the waistband of Jordan's shorts. "We can still make it happen. How's your bear growl?" Jordan's shorts fell down his legs, leaving him in just his generic brand gray boxer briefs. "We could film fan content together if you want."

Jordan swallowed hard, uncomfortable with their closeness. "I'm not doing porn. I'll leave that to the real actors like you."

Billy took Jordan by the hand and pulled him into the bed. "Okay, but no more being ashamed of your body with me." Billy curled up into Jordan and draped Jordan's arm around him, so they were spooning. "You never have to be ashamed of anything with me, okay?"

Jordan pulled the sheet over them. He inhaled the smell of Billy's shampoo. "Okay. Good night."

"Sweet dreams. Good night." Billy reached over and turned the light out.

GLORY HOLEALUJAH

CLOSING HIS EYES, Billy took a deep breath and let it out slowly. He was getting in the mindset of the scene. This was all action, no talking. He really didn't have a reference point to this type of scene. They didn't have gloryholes where he came from, at least none that he was aware of. It wasn't until he did porn that he even experienced one.

Billy took another deep breath. This time, when he let out the breath, he opened his eyes. With nerves as steady as steel, he opened the door to the fake public bathroom. Stepping through, he became his character: Gloryhole Slut, a young man so horny and in need of cock he'd gone to this known hook up spot.

The set was a somewhat realistic public bathroom. The three actual walls were a marbleized powder blue and white. The singular toilet stall right there as he opened the door was made out of cheap plywood painted a muted gray. This set was all-too familiar. Billy had seen several of the videos and the set rarely changed.

Billy walked around the reasonable facsimile stall to the pristine singular urinal by its sink-and-mirror counterpart. On this side of the stall was a door-knob-size hole, perfectly placed to allow his co-star to shove his cock through. Billy knew they moved the wall up and down for the vertically challenged actors.

Billy sidled up to the urinal and undid his shorts. Glancing over at the hole in the wall, Billy pulled out his cock and began stroking himself hard. Licking his lips, Billy imagined the excitement and danger guys must have felt using these. He could see the lure of it, though he doubted he'd do it in real life.

Without pissing, he tucked his hard cock back into his shorts. Leaving his shorts undid, he walked around and into the stall. Shutting the door, he dropped his shorts and sat on the cold porcelain. He mentally counted to fifteen, wondering if people still actually did this sort of thing in public.

The door opened again, and the booted feet of Derek came into view under the stall. Billy watched them move around the stall and up to the urinal. Billy leaned forward and looked through the gloryhole at Derek's eight-inch-thick dark meat sticking out of his pants, hard and ready.

Derek was a good six inches taller than Billy and had at least a hundred pounds on him. Aside from Derek being black with smooth, cocoa-brown skin and a closely trimmed fade, he reminded Billy of Jordan. They had the same body, basically: cubbish with muscle, but not really fat. Billy suspected that

even Derek's cock was similar to Jordan's. He hadn't
seen Jordan's, but he felt it last night.

Billy put two fingers through the hole, running
them around the edges before pulling them back so
he could look through again. He watched Derek look
around, pretending to be nervous while he started
stroking his cock. He turned to present his cock to
Billy, then slipped his dick through the hole.

Billy gripped it in his hand, feeling the heat and
the needing throb for release in his palm. He took the
cock in his mouth as he slipped off the toilet onto his
knees. Closing his eyes, Billy sucked and played with
the head, running his tongue under the crown before
taking the first few inches down.

With the wall separating them, they could both
pretend the other person was someone different.
Billy didn't know who Derek was thinking of, but
he was thinking of Jordan. He pretended those low
moans from Derek were actually coming from Jordan,
attempting to be quiet and not let loose.

Needing the man to moan louder for him, Billy
started running his tongue along the underside of
Derek's shaft. He pressed his face into the hole—into
Derek's crotch—and the scent of Derek's soap filled
Billy's nostrils. It was the same scent he smelled
on Jordan after he showered. Billy pulled off and
stroked the faceless cock, bringing himself back into
the moment. He remembered he shouldn't think of
Jordan that way.

He did anyway.

Derek pulled back from the hole, his cock sliding
through Billy's gripping fingers. Derek dropped to

his knees now, mouth open at the hole. It took Billy a moment to realize he was playing a part, but he stood and pushed his own ten inches through the hole. Billy pulled off his shirt and tossed it on top of the toilet tank.

When Derek's hot mouth surrounded his cock, Billy envisioned it was Jordan. This hungry mouth exploring his cock was Jordan's, wanting to memorize every vein and bump on Billy's cock. Billy reached up and grabbed the top of the wall before slowly humping his cock into the hole and into the warm wet mouth on the other side. He wondered if Jordan liked it rough, or gentle, if Jordan had any kinks or if he was adventurous in bed.

Derek pulled off Billy's cock and stood up. Billy turned as the makeshift stall door opened. He half expected it to be Jordan, but it was a shirtless Derek, cock pointed at Billy like a sexual divining rod. He pulled Billy from the stall, Billy leaving his shorts on the floor. They moved around to the open space where the urinal and sink resided.

With a hand on his shoulder, Derek pushed Billy down to his knees and back onto his cock. Billy groaned, closing his eyes when Derek ran his hands through his hair. He remembered Jordan playing with his hair last night and how much he liked it when Jordan touched him. It was always skittish, yet tender.

Derek shoved his pants farther down his thighs. With his hands fisting Billy's hair, Derek humped into his mouth. Billy relaxed his mouth, letting Derek use it. He reached up and around, grabbing Derek's firm, yet soft ass. He imagined Jordan's ass feeling like this—plush and tight, perfect for sinking into, or just casually putting his hand on as they walked down the street.

Derek pulled out and Billy knew what to do. He got on all fours, presenting his lubed-up ass to Derek. Derek grabbed Billy's hips roughly. *Thank God I used that toy to stretch out,* Billy thought as Derek sank balls-deep into him. For the camera, he grunted and pretended to wince in pain.

Derek slapped his hips into Billy repeatedly, at a casually fast pace designed to prolong the experience. Billy moaned and groaned, reaching under himself to stroke himself in time with the thrusts. Derek put a hand on the small of his back, silently telling Billy to arch his back more. He did, tossing his head back with a stifled groan.

Derek pulled out and got on his back, pants bunched up around his ankles. Billy straddled him, with one hand behind him to steady his descent, the other holding his cock and balls out of the way of the shot of Derek's cock disappearing into him. Billy bit his lip, more from the slow strain of his muscles than the cock penetrating him.

Derek took hold of Billy's slender hips and guided him to bounce up and down while Billy stroked his own dick. Billy closed his eyes. He thought about Jordan and his bed that creaked whenever they moved on it. He thought about the sounds it would make if they took their new friendship into even newer territory. Billy imagined the bed would probably break.

The next thing Billy knew he was on his back, legs in the air and his ankles framing Derek's sweet face.

He didn't stop stroking his cock as Derek pumped furiously into him. Planting his hands on either side of Billy, Derek leaned down pressing Billy's legs to his chest and giving the camera the perfect view of Derek's cock slamming into his hole.

Billy looked up into Derek's intense sensitive eyes. They were so much like Jordan's. "You're going to make me cum, Jordan," Billy whispered softly. Then, three more strokes of his dick, and he was doing just that. His cock exploded, shooting ropes of white across his defined abs and chest.

Once Billy's convulsing orgasm subsided, Derek pulled out and stroked his cock over Billy's. Billy watched his sex face: the gritting of Derek's teeth, the intense look when Derek climaxed. He added his own white splatters to join Billy's across his chest and stomach. The last little dribbles landed on Billy's balls.

There was no ceremony at the ending of this encounter. Derek simply got up, tucked his cock back in his pants, grabbed his shirt and left Billy there, covered in their spunk. Billy stretched out, running his hands through the white on his body. He'd make Jordan cum inside him if they ever went that far. Pulling out was for porn.

CHEETAH SPOTS

BRETT LAID IN bed going through pictures. When Chris came by to check up on him, he asked if Sean was coming over. Chris gave that familiar disapproving look when Brett told him Sean was with his wife and kid. Chris never approved of their "special arrangement" relationship.

They didn't understand that Brett was okay with Sean slipping into his bed at three in the morning after drinking at some strip club with his boys, or coming in for an "oil change," and so Brett could dip his stick in Sean. That was good enough for Brett. He had done the trappings of a real relationship with Shadow. Shadow abandoned him. Now, he was wondering if Shadow even thought about him. If Shadow was alive or dead.

Brett looked at the picture in front of him: Shadow, Joe, Mario, and Billy. The original true Country Boyz. It was taken right after Billy's initiation into escorting. Kevin and Keith were absent, having left for college;

they never came back to film. He heard rumors they were doing their own thing at school, making fan content. That moment was the beginning of the end.

Brett remembered that Saturday morning in August. Mario and Randy had just started purchasing their home. Everything seemed perfect between him and Shadow. Joe was his normal gruff self, making them breakfast every morning.

Billy stormed in, red-faced and angry, and they all knew why. Billy had caught the eye of the locally closeted Congressman, and Brett had finally relented to letting him have a night with Billy.

"You fucking bastards! You could have told me!" Billy yelled, storming in the kitchen.

"About what? His cheetah spots?" Mario asked, lips pressed into a tight smile to keep from laughing.

Billy continued his rant. "I came out of the bathroom, and he was on all fours on the bed waiting for me! There were these black spots all over his ass! I almost threw up! I went back into the bathroom, grabbed a washcloth, and tried to wipe them off!"

"Did they? Come off, that is?" Shadow asked, his chest bouncing from holding in the laughter.

Billy glared at them. "I kept wiping and wiping trying to get them off. Then he said, and I quote, 'Those are moles. My mama called them my cheetah spots.' He needs to get those things removed!" Everyone erupted in laughter.

"What did you do after that?" Mario asked, eyes watering from laughing.

Billy was trying not to laugh now. "The only thing I could do. I turned the lights off and closed my eyes."

Laughter erupted again. "It's not funny!" Billy yelled, trying not to laugh.

"They've all had similar experiences. It's a rite of passage around here. Even Kevin and Keith had their turn," Joe chuckled.

Shadow rolled his eyes. "Keith just shoved it in like the straight boy he is. Kevin put on a blind fold and made our illustrious political representative ride him."

"Isn't it a little hypocritical of him hiring us as escorts? Especially with all the anti-gay legislation he supports?" Billy asked, joining in the laughter.

Mario shrugged. "Money is money. He pays good money, and we've got bills to pay."

Billy sat down at the kitchen table. "Yeah, I get that, but his money feels … I don't know … dirty."

Joe sat a plate of sausage and bacon in the middle of the table. "It is. If we try to out him, it could hurt us more. That man has ties and connections which could easily end us. Literally."

"Not to mention the other high-profile people who wouldn't use us to escort. It's something we have to do in this line of work, put aside our personal feelings," Shadow added, grabbing bacon from the plate.

Brett sipped his coffee. "To the world we're nothing but dirty whores having sex for money. They fuck us in private and look down their nose at us in public."

Billy started scooping scrambled eggs off the plate as Joe sat down in front of him. Billy contemplated, "I don't see why. We provide a service that is so obviously needed. I mean, without us, a lot of men wouldn't have anything to jack-off to, let alone get laid."

Mario was nibbling on a piece of bacon. "Because we're a fantasy. They don't like to admit that we are what they really want in their reality. Why do you think they have me dress up in a wig and a dress?"

Joe sat beside Billy. "Not to mention the financial hit the Country Boyz site, and we would take from the lawsuits if we tried to out him. They'd bankrupt us into silence. Face it, Billy: we're small fish trying not to get eaten by the bigger ones."

Billy pouted. "It just doesn't seem right or fair, especially with everything over the past few years."

Mario speared a sausage and waved it at Billy. "Honey, if I'm dressed as Maria in a bar and a guy gets handsy and finds out I have an outie instead of an innie, I could end up dead."

Joe scooped eggs onto his plate and added, "When I was growing up, you could get fired for being gay. You couldn't serve in the military, and people were calling AIDS God's punishment for sin." Billy stared, wide-eyed at Joe. "That was a step up from the older gays that told me their stories."

Billy looked around the table. "But we've come so far. Right?"

Joe closed his eyes and stated, "We have, and we have so much further to go. You'll see one day when you do something like date a black guy, or a drag queen, or someone that isn't the gay social norm."

Billy looked at Joe in awe. "You dated a black drag queen? You have *so* got to tell me about him … err … her."

Joe laughed. "Carlton wasn't a drag queen. He was as sassy as one, but he wasn't a drag queen. He was black, though."

"What happened?" Billy dropped his fork, intently listening to Joe.

"The white gays called me a 'chocolate-chaser.' That was one of the less offensive names. The black Gays called Carlton names I won't repeat." Joe took a deep breath before he continued, "Billy, you've lived a sheltered, privileged life. When you finally get exposed to all the hate in this world—even from our own—promise me you won't let it jade you like it did me."

Billy put a comforting hand on Joe's. "I promise. What happened to you and Carlton?"

There were tears in Joe's eyes. "He left me after his family found out. I don't know what upset them more: that he was gay or sleeping with a white devil." Joe looked at Billy. "He runs a small law firm two counties over. I saw him once … with his wife and kid."

Billy squeezed Joe's hand. "It hurt, didn't it? When it happens to me, will you be there for me?"

Scrambled eggs hit Billy's face. "We'll all be there for you. Now quit ruining breakfast. I want to tell everyone about my date last night. He was so lame! Billy, do you think you would ever put on a dress and wig to help me out with these…" and then, while making air quotes with his fingers, Mario finished, "heterosexual men?"

Billy laughed. "I would look like a boy in a dress. Where did Mr. Lame take you last night?"

Brett sighed and rolled over, finally looking away from the picture. Closing his eyes against the filtered daylight, he let sleep take him over. He wasn't tired, but the events of the past twenty-four hours took their toll on him. He wanted to wake up in a few hours to find this was all a horrible nightmare and Mario and Joe were still alive.

Brett didn't wake up, though. He might have, had he heard the cautious footsteps of the person who opened his trailer door and blew out his pilot light. He may have woken up, if he had smelled the gas slowly filling his single-wide trailer, the gas which crept in through Brett's nose and mouth, filling his lungs and spreading through his body ... sending Brett into a slumber from which he'd never wake up.

SWEET, SWEET FANTASY

JORDAN SAT AT his desk with his headset on, scrolling through the notes on the account as the woman on his phone continued to rant about how her phone was hacked. He sighed, letting the woman prattle on and on. He just wanted to scream at her, "You're not that important! You can't even pay your bill! You have a flip phone!"

Instead, he leaned back in his chair and looked at his bed, the bed he shared with Billy for the past few nights and probably would be sharing with him for the foreseeable future. They were sharing it just as friends. Friends without benefits. If only they had those benefits and were more than just friends.

Jordan closed his eyes. The woman screeching "they're listening to my phone calls!" faded away, and he let his mind drift. His imagination mixed with his desire, and the seeds of a fantasy began to form. It was just a tiny thought, but soon it grew. He could see it, so easily … Billy and him.

In Jordan's mind, he saw Billy on the couch, his smooth, toned body on full display. Billy lay on his stomach wearing only those form-fitting green briefs. Jordan loved how just the bottom of Billy's plump ass hung out and the material clung to him like a second skin. The delectable sight would be too much for Jordan not to act.

Jordan would walk up wearing only a pair of jeans—shirtless—gliding his fingers up Billy's leg. Billy would prop himself up on his elbow and turn to look at him. Then, Jordan would drop to his knees beside Billy, his hand moving up under Billy's briefs to feel the hard firm cheeks. Silent consent to go on would be in Billy's eyes.

He would lean in and kiss Billy's chest, his hand gently squeezing Billy's ass. Billy would turn and kiss on his exposed neck. He would then turn and catch Billy's mouth with his own. The kiss, sensual and soft, would be mere moments, but the memory of it would last an eternity.

He then would move down along Billy's body, tasting it with gentle seductive kisses. He would pull up the bottom of Billy's briefs, exposing the cheek for him to adorn it with grazes from his lips. The fabric would bunch up between Billy's cheeks, preventing Jordan from exploring further, but he'd kiss and suck the supple skin, giving Billy a hint of what was to come.

Billy would moan, arching his body at the soft press of Jordan's lips on his skin, and when Jordan finally pulled the briefs down, Billy would move his body so they would slide easily off. Billy's body would tremble with need and anticipation for something they both had wanted since the first time they met.

He would lean down, part Billy's perfect cheeks and run his tongue over the pink flesh. He imagined Billy would taste like fun, smiles, and laughter. Billy's hand would reach back and grip Jordan's shoulder, then run over his body … and Jordan would continue to slowly binge on Billy's intoxicating flavor.

Jordan would move back up to Billy's quivering lips. Kissing him, he would slip his middle finger into Billy and finger-fuck him, making Billy moan into his mouth. Jordan's index finger would slide in along to join with the first. A soft grunt escaping Billy in response to the pleasurable stretch, Billy's hand would reach down to Jordan's, guiding him to finger-fuck him even harder.

Jordan's fingers would slip from Billy's ass as he would guide Billy to sit, their kiss never breaking until Jordan lifted Billy's legs and pressed them to his chest. Putting Billy on his back, his cock, balls, and hole would be on full display for Jordan. The sight would be a thing of beauty and a feast on which he'd gorge himself.

Jordan would let go of the legs when Billy hooked his arms under them. He'd run his appreciative hand over Billy's smooth cheeks, a cautiously delicate touch reserved for handling a work of art. The touch Billy longed for. The touch Billy craved from only Jordan.

Soft murmurs would escape Billy, and Jordan would see his own want and lust mirrored in Billy's face. Tender kisses would be planted on the cheeks, watching Billy shudder with anticipation. Before he'd

go in for the coup de grace, Jordan would stretch his body up to kiss Billy's mouth, their tongues sliding along one another in a graceful ballet.

Leaving them both wanting more, Jordan would lower himself back down between Billy's legs. He'd run a light finger over Billy's pink pucker, stroking the tight ring. Billy would let out a soft moan that would turn into a gasp when Jordan leaned in and slowly ran his tongue in circles around Billy's hole.

When Billy couldn't take anymore—and his breath quick with desire—Jordan would zero-in, darting his tongue rapidly into Billy, only to suddenly stop and return to slow circles and the occasional teasing swipe of his tongue. Billy would be worked up again, and Jordan's tongue would quickly strike again.

He would occasionally move up to kiss Billy, quieting the building sexual storm for just a moment longer. But, back between Billy's legs, Jordan would stir that storm back into a frenzy. His own cock would be hard and pressing against his jeans, desperate for escape ... desperate to spring free and sink into Billy.

When Billy expected the long, languid lick along his crevice to culminate into another kiss, Jordan would pause to take one of Billy's balls in his mouth ... first one and then the other. Their fullness and eagerness to burst would weigh heavy on his tongue. He'd swap them over and over, making Billy mewl with urgency.

Releasing the precious orbs, he would flick his tongue up Billy's hard shaft to the flared head leaking tiny lakes into the valleys of Billy's stomach. He'd take the head of Billy's cock in his mouth, and tasting the sweetness of his soul, Jordan would look into Billy's eyes to see the conflicting pleas to both continue and stop.

Jordan would nurse just the tip for a bit before slowly gorging himself on the full ten inches. Billy would barely notice the slip of two of Jordan's fingers into him, and Jordan would feel around inside of him looking for his sweet spot. Finding it, he would repeat those mind-numbing, slow circles with his fingertips over Billy's prostate.

This would send Billy into an almost uncontrollable frenzy, thrusting his cock deep into Jordan's mouth then back down onto Jordan's exploring fingers. He would cup Billy's bouncing balls, feeling for when Billy's detonator almost struck zero. Right at the cusp, he would pull off and out of Billy. His mouth would cover Billy's, quieting the cries of the denial of his orgasm.

Billy would release his legs, letting them fall to either side of Jordan. The now-free arms would wrap around Jordan, holding him there until Billy's near-boil calmed to a slow simmer. Billy's hands would then push Jordan up onto his feet—Jordan would be leaning down to continue their ravenous kisses while both men would work to free Jordan's cock from its denim prison.

This is when they'd break the kiss, allowing Jordan to discard the villainous garment. He'd stand between Billy's legs. His hard, seven inches jutting out from his dark-trimmed pubes under his slight stomach. He would keep his promise to Billy and wouldn't be ashamed of his body. Billy wanted him. Wanted him as he was.

Billy's warm, inviting mouth would engulf Jordan, his hand roaming all over him. Billy would explore the body he'd been curled up next to—night after night—but was too scared to truly touch. He'd play with Jordan's tiny nipples, move along to cup his full ass, trail down to run through the dark hair on his legs, then back up to play in the burgeoning forest on Jordan's chest.

With a caressing hand, Jordan would cup Billy's chin and pull Billy off his cock. Leaning down to kiss Billy again, he'd guide Billy onto his back once more, pinning Billy's legs to his chest. Billy folded in half, Jordan's cock would brush up and down Billy's spit-slick hole.

There would be muffled cries of dismay as Jordan's cock passed over Billy's entrance but did not enter. Over and over, Jordan's cock would tease them both being so *close*, but not entering … then, with a slight change of his hips, the head of Jordan's dick would pop in. Wanting Jordan inside him—*needing* Jordan inside him—Billy would pull him in welcomingly until his balls rested against Billy's ass.

Tongues tangling and hands exploring, the two would be locked in a steady, affectionate, slow hump. Both would want it harder and faster, but neither would want to give up the slow pleasurable indulgence of their first time. This time, this first time, was one that they wanted to last forever.

Pulling back and out of Billy, Jordan would pull Billy up to standing. Insatiable, Billy would take

charge by kissing him while pushing Jordan back onto the couch. Billy would climb up on the couch—legs on either side of Jordan—and spearing himself on Jordan's cock, Billy would lower himself down until he rested on Jordan's thighs.

Billy would pull them back into a passionate kiss as he rode Jordan's dick. Jordan would thrust up, meeting Billy, and his hand would wrap around Billy's cock, pumping him as they pistoned like a well-oiled machine.

Sweat would glisten off their bodies as they synchronized. Billy's cock would throb in his hand. Jordan's cock would throb in Billy's ass. Soon, the most spectacular moment would occur for them both. Together, they'd cry out into the kiss, Billy sucking on his bottom lip as they both released a tsunami of pent-up sexual tension... Billy across Jordan's stomach, Jordan deep inside Billy.

They'd fall over together, Jordan's cock slipping from Billy as they lay side-by-side on the couch. Billy would nuzzle close to him. He would hold Billy close, protecting him from the world. They would lay like that, casually kissing and cuddling, and it would be the perfect moment of bliss and contentment.

The shrill voice brought Jordan back to the present. "Are you listening to me?! Hello? Did you hang up?"

Jordan rolled his eyes, adjusting his hard-on. "No, ma'am. I'm still here."

"Well, I want a credit for the services I can't use because of those hackers! Your company should be doing more to help me!"

Jordan gritted his teeth, then explained with practiced patience, "Ma'am, you can't use your services because you were disconnected for non-payment three months ago." The line went dead.

Jordan logged out for a personal moment. He looked over at the bed, wondering if fantasy could ever be a reality. Maybe one day.

16

THE NOT-BOYFRIEND-BOYFRIEND

BILLY LIKED **DEREK.** He was nice, friendly, and down-to-Earth. They took photos together after the shoot and posted them on their respective social media. They made plans to shoot together for fan content later in the week when both of their schedules aligned. Billy hoped this would be the beginning of many West Coast friendships. He needed to lay down roots here if he was going to stay.

"So, who is Jordan?" Derek asked, typing away at his phone.

"Jordan? No one. Why do you ask?" Billy questioned while also typing on his phone, feeling his cheeks flush a little.

Derek set his phone down. "You moaned his name a few times. Is that the 'special someone' in your life?"

Billy tried to laugh it off, keeping his eyes locked on his phone to keep from giving away the lie. "No, he's my neighbor. I recently met him, and we've been hanging out all the time. We're buds, you know?"

"I see. So, you two haven't gone out on any dates or slept with each other?" Derek clarified suspiciously, picking back up his phone.

"Of course not. I mean, we have *slept* together—every single night since we met—but all we did was sleep," Billy blurted.

"Has he cooked you dinner?" Derek asked, raising an eyebrow while continuing to scroll his phone.

Billy answered sheepishly, "No, I cooked him dinner."

Derek held up his phone displaying one of the many pictures Billy had taken with Jordan. "Is this him? He's cute."

Billy smiled shyly. "Yes. And yes, he is cute."

"So, what's stopping you from taking it to the next level? You obviously like him. You moaned his name a couple times during filming." Billy looked down at his feet. "Oh, he's not in the industry or he doesn't know you do porn."

Billy sat his phone down and finally looked at Derek. "He knows I do porn and doesn't care. He was a fan before I met him."

Derek leaned forward, resting his elbows on his knees. "Pardon the euphemism, but let me get this straight... He knows you do porn and doesn't care. You spend just about every waking moment with him, sleep in the same bed and haven't done anything. You made him dinner, and you moaned his name a couple times today."

Billy added, "And yesterday I bought us groceries. While we were watching TV, I had my head in his lap, and he was playing with my hair."

Derek leaned back, laughing. "Boy, you got it bad for him, and you just don't see it, do you?"

"I do not," Billy huffed defiantly. "We're just really good friends, and I'm helping him with his writing career." Billy's face brightened at his last thought and said, "You should read the funny script he wrote about me."

"Hey, babe. I'm done with my scene. Are you ready to go?" They both turned their attention to the bright-eyed, slender, black man in a tight tee displaying his muscular form.

Derek stood and gave the sexy man a kiss. "Just a minute. Billy, this is my husband, Drake. Drake, this is Billy. We're going to film content later this week."

Drake extended his hand. "Pleasure to meet you. It's always nice to meet the men having sex with my husband."

Billy stood and took the offered hand. "The pleasure is mine. I always like meeting the people who break in the men before I get them."

"Billy was telling me his not-boyfriend-boyfriend wrote him a funny script. Remember when *you* were not my not-boyfriend-boyfriend?" Derek nudged Drake.

Drake rolled his eyes. "We were living together for six months, and it was coming up on our one-year anniversary. I asked him what he wanted to do for the big day, and do you know what this sexy bastard said?" Drake playfully punched Derek. "He said, 'What anniversary?' He didn't even realize I moved in!"

Derek laughed. "When I told my mom, she said, 'baby, I knew that months ago.' The entire world knew, except me."

Drake hugged Derek. "You knew in your heart." Then, Drake turned his attention back to Billy and asked, "Are you going to Lexi's party Friday?"

"Lexi the director? No, I wasn't invited." Billy felt a pang of shame. Back East he was one of the first invited to every party and event because he'd networked and made connections. He hadn't done any of those since coming out West.

"Well, I'm inviting you and your not-boy-friend-boyfriend. I want to check him out," Drake teased, winking at Billy.

"Oh, he's cute. See?" Derek held his phone up for Drake to see the picture of Billy and Jordan together.

Drake drew out the words as he studied the picture, "He … is… *thick* like a biscuit, too."

"If you don't want him, we'll take him. Ouch!" Derek rubbed his arm where Drake pinched him.

"Let's go before you get yourself in more trouble," Drake said, extending his hand to Billy again. "It's been a pleasure, Billy. I can't wait to meet your not-boyfriend-boyfriend."

Billy took the offered hand and replied, "Jordan. His name is Jordan."

126

SITTING ON THE DOCK

KEITH SAT AT the edge of the dock, legs dangling, bare feet hanging just above the water of the lake. He took another swig from his can of beer. He couldn't believe this was happening to him. He'd left work at lunch and hadn't gone back. He couldn't, not after what they saw.

Downing the last of his beer, Keith reached into the cooler to pull out another. He didn't know why he was drinking, other than he didn't know what else to do. It wouldn't wipe away the memory of everyone who saw those videos and pictures. It wouldn't wipe away the pain and embarrassment. It wouldn't change the fact his life was essentially ruined.

It did dull the pain, however.

The mail must have been delivered right as he sat down to lunch that day in the law firm for which he was interning. Whoever did this had done their research. Each envelope was personally addressed to every person in the law firm. Each envelope contained a collage of pictures of Keith from the Country Boyz web site showing everything from getting his dicked sucked to eating and fucking ass.

It hadn't stopped there. Keith sat stunned in the restaurant as Sheila from Human Resources explained, "It was sent to every judge and law firm in the state, from what we can tell." Keith slammed his fist on the table, scaring away the server who came to take his order. "Our phones have been ringing nonstop." Shelia paused. "The law firm's logo and contact info is printed on it with the words, 'We're proud of our new intern.'"

"I'll skip lunch and come back to the office," Keith said immediately. Panicked, he stood quickly, hitting the table and spilling the neglected complimentary water. "Shit!"

"Keith…" he heard Sheila say into his ear.

"Can I get some fucking towels over here?!" Keith shouted angrily into the quiet restaurant. All eyes were on him. A brave server came over with towels and began soaking up the spilled water. *Thank you*, he mouthed to the server. "I'm sorry, Sheila. I had a bit of an accident. I'll be back in the office soon."

"Keith," Sheila repeated his name more insistently this time. Keith sank down in the chair. "That's what I've been trying to tell you. Don't come back to the office. We're packing up your personal things now. You've been let go. I just need to know where you want me to send them."

Notifications began to pummel his phone. The group text he shared with his fraternity brothers was the first of the flood, the rest followed by his family and friends. Some of them had also received thumb drives with every scene he had performed at Country Boyz.

What the fuck dude? began the thread with his frat.

It's all over campus!

I didn't know you were a fag, man!

We showered together! Were you checking me out??!!

It went on like that until the fraternity president intervened. *Delete this thread. I'm starting a new group chat WITHOUT Keith.*

Then, he went to the messages from his girlfriend. *WTF! You're gay??!! I just got a USB drive full of videos of you fucking all these dudes! Did you ever like me?! No wonder you always wanted to do anal!*

The worst and most terrifying came from his father. It simply said, *Call me. NOW.*

He ignored the rest of the messages. Standing up and walking out of the restaurant with all eyes on him, he couldn't help but wonder if they had all seen the pictures or videos on their phones. His hands were trembling, and his face had flushed red. He struggled to catch his breath all the way back to his SUV.

He tried not to cry as he made the first phone call. "Dad, I know it's bad."

The disappointment in his father's voice killed Keith, "Son, everyone at my work and our church received mail containing pictures of you doing lewd and un-Godly things today. Your mother has been getting calls from everyone at the church asking why we would tolerate such sin in our home."

Keith hung his head in shame. Defeated, he said, "Dad, it went to everyone at my work, too. I was fired. What am I going to do?"

"You should have thought about that before you sinned," his father retorted, his voice a mix of shame and hate.

Tears began falling down Keith's cheeks as he pleaded, "Dad … I … I can explain. I'll just come home and—"

His father cut him off, "Don't you dare come home. Go to the cabin at the lake until this blows over. Your mother and I will do what we can to manage this. Maybe tell them you went to one of those rehabilitation places."

"Dad, I'm not gay."

His father ignored his comment. "Just go to the lake house. We'll do damage control."

Finished with that conversation, he stopped at the local convenience store and loaded his SUV up with all the beer he could carry. The clerk ringing him up flirtatiously asked if he was throwing a party, to which he snarled angrily, "Just ring me up, fag."

Luckily, there wasn't any cell service at the house. Those menacing notifications tormenting him stopped coming. He knew they were still present, looming over him, waiting in the darkness of Cyberspace for just a hint of signal, so they could rain down on him like Hellfire.

"Why did I do it?" he asked the night sky.

He knew why; he had a hot body, a big cock, liked to be ogled, and liked to fuck. His parents were always ragging on him not to get a girl pregnant, and he hated condoms. What else was he supposed to do? He did what any other horny young man would do: he found a guy who could take care of his needs.

That's why—since high school—he and Kevin were such good friends. He kept Kevin's cover, and Kevin kept his balls drained. That was their arrangement. When Kevin came to him about filming stuff with these guys he met at some trashy gay bar, Keith should have said "no" instead of getting excited about the idea.

He remembered Kevin trying to convince him, saying, "No one will ever see it. We can make a little extra money for beer. It'll be fun."

He downed the rest of his beer and said aloud to himself, "You didn't need convincing, did you? You fucking idiot." Keith stood up on wobbly legs. He fumbled with the front of his pants to pull out his cock. "You're the reason I'm in this mess," he accused. The pressure on his bladder eased with the hot stream of piss that shot out.

He stumbled back, then lurched forward, nearly falling into the water. Keith tucked his cock away. "Fuck. You're going to be the death of me." Keith turned around to walk back to the house.

He squinted at the shadowy figure in the darkness. "Who the fuck are you?"

Those were Keith's last words before the bat hit him in the temple and sent him crashing to the deck. He looked up briefly, head throbbing, mind foggy from alcohol and the hit. His eyes grew heavy. He reached out to the figure standing over him, but his hand fell to the deck as his eyes closed.

He was aware of the hands on him, the hands that rolled him across the dock and over the edge into the lake. He felt the cold water as it surrounded his body. *Swim!* he thought, but his arms and legs did nothing. He opened his mouth to scream only to have water fill his mouth. He choked and coughed. Water filled his lungs. *Swim!* he thought again before he just gave up and let the darkness take him.

18

PULLING OUT IS FOR PORN

JORDAN SAT IN the laundry room watching his clothes tumble with Billy's. He really needed to talk to Billy about what they were doing. The lines of their friendship seemed to blur as more time was spent together. The only thing they didn't do that a normal couple did was have sex. However, given what he heard from his friends in current relationships, that was normal, too.

Billy had basically moved in with him. They spent all their free time together. Jordan couldn't even imagine what it would be like now to fall asleep *without* Billy in his arms. Now, he was doing Billy's laundry with his own while Billy was at his last shoot for the week. Billy had a fan content shoot with Derek and Drake on Wednesday, but then that was it for Billy this week.

Yesterday, when Billy arrived home from the studio, he came straight over to Jordan's. Jordan still had two more hours before his shift ended, so to occupy himself, Billy did the unimaginable: he cleaned. Not only did he clean, he also made dinner. He half-suspected Billy was up to something.

It wasn't just a normal let-me-wipe-things-down-cleaning; it was a full-blown pick-things-up-and-dust, move-the-furniture-to-chase-away-the-dust-bunnies, if-the-place-doesn't-smell-like-lemon-and-pine-start-over-again-cleaning. Had Jordan not stepped out of his own bedroom, he would have thought he was in the wrong apartment.

In true 1950's housewife fashion, Billy pulled out a warming plate from the oven, set it on the kitchen table, then came over and kissed him on the cheek. The only thing missing was Billy dressed in an apron holding the trademark chilled, three-olive martini. Jordan could do without the martini, but Billy wearing only an apron… now *that* would be a sight he wouldn't mind.

Billy sat Jordan down at the table, then disappeared into the bedroom yelling over his shoulder in a chipper voice, "Eat while I clean the bedroom!"

Jordan thought to himself, *I have a porn star cleaning my apartment, cooking me dinner, and sharing my bed.* When Billy asked if he would do the laundry, what could Jordan say? Hence, Jordan sitting in the laundry room, watching the clothes tumble in the dryer, laughing to himself at the irony that someone who made a living by being naked owned so much laundry.

He remembered the first time he saw Billy in a video. He couldn't recall the name of the other guy, but Jordan remembered Billy's sweet innocent cherub face and delicious smooth body on his computer screen. Every time he visited that memory, he placed himself as the other young, hard body opposite Billy.

In his mind, Jordan had the perfect porn star body. This changed with his taste, but right now he imagined himself a smooth, young twink. Billy and he were sitting cross-legged on the bed, shirtless, and in the shortest shorts one could wear and still be considered decent. They were playing video games, playfully nudging each other to try and make the other lose.

Billy nudged him. "I'm going to win."

"No, you're not!" Jordan knocked back.

"Want to bet?" Billy asked, right before reaching over and snatching the controller out of Jordan's hand.

He lunged at Billy, knocking him onto his back and yelling, "Cheater!"

Mysteriously, the controllers would be gone, and he would be on top of Billy, their matching smooth, slender bodies pressed together as they wrestled playfully on the bed. They would keep trying to pin each other's arms, rolling around with their shorts bunching up and riding up between their respective ass cheeks.

"Surrender!" Billy claimed triumphantly, sitting on top of Jordan and holding his hands down on the bed. Their hard crotches pressed together.

Pretending to struggle under Billy, he would cry out, "Never!"

Billy would start grinding his crotch into his. He'd look intently into Jordan's eyes. He'd bring his face close to Jordan's, noses almost touching. Billy would say in a soft whisper, "Surrender ... and I'll fuck you."

His chest would be heaving, the sensual moment lasting longer than it should in any modern porn. He'd answer back in a lustful whisper, "I surrender."

Keeping Jordan's hands pinned to the bed, Billy would kiss him. Not a fast and furious, let's-get-naked-and-fuck kiss, but a slow, sensual kiss he would feel through his entire body that curled his toes. A kiss that satisfied all his sexual needs while simultaneously sending them into overdrive.

Billy's grip on Jordan's wrists would relax. With a feather touch, Billy's fingers would move down his arms. One deep kiss later, Billy would move down Jordan's body, kissing and sucking along the path from his mouth … down his neck … farther down through the middle of Jordan's chest…

Billy would linger at Jordan's stomach; it would be concave, pulled tight and taut from his breath hitched in his chest. Billy's fingers would join his mouth on the journey, moving down Jordan's sides until they found the top of his shorts. Billy would slightly tug. A tease, but not a fulfillment of that which was to come.

"To the victor goes the spoils!" Billy would proclaim and sit up on his knees between Jordan's spread legs. He'd let Billy strip him.

Jordan's impossibly hard, youthful cock would thump hard against his belly. Tossing the tiny shorts aside, Billy would reach out to cradle his cock. Lifting it to the sky like a mighty rocket, Billy would pump it once, twice, three times before covering the glistening head with his mouth.

"Damn, Billy. I should lose more often," Jordan would moan, pushing his hips up. Jordan would bring a hand down to run his hands through the carefully sculpted, wild hair.

Jordan could imagine the feeling of Billy's tongue fondling his cock as Billy slowly worked his mouth up and down his shaft during his fantasy. Billy would take his balls in one hand, carefully playing with them while the other hand roamed up the center of Jordan's chest. Billy would run his hands over his perfect pecs.

Jordan would cry out softly, "Oh, Billy. Billy... oh God, Billy," as Billy was the one in charge, here. Billy would bring his hand down, scraping his nails lightly over Jordan's chest. "Billy," he would mew, arching his hips up and shoving his cock up into Billy's gullet.

Billy's hands would slip under Jordan's legs. He knew what was coming when Billy pulled off his cock. Jordan's legs would be lifted and pushed back to his chest. He would wrap his arms under his own legs to hold them there and present his hole to Billy. Billy would put his hands on Jordan's ass, fingers splayed to frame his pucker.

Moving in, Billy would run a tongue around his hole. The anticipation would build in Jordan, as Billy's tongue would come closer and closer until it was slowly stroking his outer ring. Teasing and pleasing, the slow build up to the inevitable Jordan wouldn't see coming.

Then it would happen, the rapid-fire flick of Billy's tongue daubing at and into Jordan's hole. Eyes rolling back in his head, he would gasp at the precise and intimate bombardment. Billy would return to the slow teasing circles and swipes, and right as he would catch his breath again, bombardment.

137

Jordan would pant during one of the brief respites, "Please, Billy, I need your cock."

Pulling back from him, Billy would say, "I need that mouth."

Jordan would drop his legs; Billy would quickly slip out of his shorts and sling his feet beside his head. That was an unspoken, directed acknowledgement for Jordan. He would straddle Billy's chest, ass precariously close to Billy's mouth, his hand wrapped around Billy's long, hard ten inches.

This was the moment Jordan dreamed about. Leaning down, he'd finally wrap his lips around the crown of Billy's cock. He'd pause there to savor the feel and taste of Billy. A coaxing gentle slap on his ass would remind Jordan to go down. He would, and with the power of fantasy, would take Billy down to his balls.

Head resting on a pillow, Billy would resume his tongue lashing. Jordan would deep-throat Billy over and over again, making Jordan moan. It wasn't the act of sucking Billy, or Billy making out with his ass which caused the moan. It would be the idea of *finally* having Billy, to give Billy back some of the pleasure he gave Jordan over the years.

He would be lost in the moment, focused solely on Billy's cock and milking his balls dry. He wouldn't even notice Billy lifting his left leg to join his, and Jordan would refuse to release Billy's cock until it was pulled from his sucking lips. A disappointment, but Jordan would know better things were coming.

Jordan would remain on all fours, while Billy moved behind him. Jordan would wiggle his ass

impatiently at Billy. With one hand on his hip and the other on his cock, Billy would lightly tap his cock on Jordan's ass. Billy would then run his crown along Jordan's spit-slicked crack, glistening it with precum.

The push of Billy's cockhead would be soft, but urgent. Jordan would easily open at the power of fantasy, and Billy would pop in. He would ease in, sink in. Like everything else, it would be slow and methodical, the quiet tease before the onslaught. Jordan would feel and enjoy that slow stretch.

Rolling his shoulders and tossing his head back, he would pant, "Billy, you feel so good in me."

And Billy would reply, "I love the way your ass feels," his voice deep and sultry.

Slowly, Billy would pull out, only a few inches. He'd push back in. Billy would repeat this over and over again, pulling out just a little more each time and increasing his speed until Billy was power-fucking him. Flesh slapping flesh, moans and groans would mix with Jordan's pleading, "Harder! Faster!"

Arms and legs trembling, Jordan would collapse onto the bed. Billy stack himself on top of him, relentlessly humping. Rolling their bodies sideways, Billy wouldn't lose momentum, and would lift his leg for a better angle while turning Jordan's head toward his and kissing him with the passion of new lovers.

They'd shift again, Billy on his back. Once again, Jordan would straddle him. He would lower himself on Billy's mighty javelin and ride him. Rising and falling on Billy, he would be stroking his own cock to near-climax. With his hands on Jordan's hips, Billy would start thrusting up.

The moment would be near and inevitable. Jordan would be first, cock erupting and shooting up to hit Billy on the chin. Volley after volley would shoot, coating Billy's chest and stomach in white. Jordan's ass would clench with the cataclysmic orgasm, putting Billy's dick in a vice and sending him over the edge.

With a tight grip on his hips, Billy would hold him there as he rapidly punched his cock up into him, Billy's balls thrown against Jordan's ass. Billy's face would change to that moment of pure need right before the bliss hit him and his cock detonated.

Now, what happened in the video and in Jordan's mind were quite different.

In the video Jordan had watched, Billy had pulled out and jerked his cock all over the guy's ass. But that was porn, and pulling out was for porn. *This* was Jordan's fantasy. In Jordan's fantasy, Billy would leave his cock inside him, pumping Jordan full of his seed… the way he wanted it in real life, the way he wanted it now.

Exhausted, Jordan would fall to the side of Billy, and Billy would pull him close, their arms and legs intertwining. They'd kiss, bodies heaving and sweaty from the exertion of it all. Nothing needed to be said because they were in that moment of jovial bliss when nothing else mattered. The moment would fade out, the scene would end.

The buzz of the drier jolted Jordan out of his fantasy. He looked around nervously to see if anyone else had joined him in the laundry room since he started taking his naughty trip down fantasy lane. Seeing no one, he adjusted himself and began pulling the clothes from the drier. With laundry secured, he headed back to his apartment. *Billy and I really need to have a talk,* he thought, wincing when the laundry basket hit his own hard basket.

ABOUT THAT...

JORDAN SUSPECTED BILLY was keeping something from him when Billy got back from filming content with Derek and Drake. He was still working, listening to yet another person who obviously never read a bill in their life, questioning every single line item they had paid for the past two years.

Billy quietly came in and began massaging Jordan's shoulders. When the tension in Jordan subsided, Billy kissed him on top of the head, then leaned down to whisper in his ear, "I'm going to make us dinner."

Dinner was over-the-top: BBQ pork chops, sweet baby carrots, Italian green beans, and a small salad which had more colors than a gay pride parade tripping on acid. After, they had store-bought cookies as dessert.

"Tomorrow, I want to go shopping for clothes after you get off work. I really want us to look good this Friday night," Billy said casually, taking their empty plates to the sink.

"I do have club-wear. It's a bit dated, but we can say it's retro or vintage," Jordan said, bringing the salad bowls.

"About that..." Billy began, which started a series of friendly arguments Jordan wouldn't win. "Derek and Drake asked if we'd go to Lexi's party with them. It's a great networking event for us."

"Lexi?"

"The porn director, Lexi Luscious. It'll be fun." Billy took the bowls from Jordan and began rinsing them.

Jordan stared wide-eyed at Billy. "Lexi Luscious? The biggest name in gay porn?"

Billy started loading the dishwasher and casually said, "Yeah."

"You go and have fun. That party is *way* out of my league."

Drying his hands, Billy turned to face Jordan. "You're going. You said you'd go out with me Friday night."

Jordan was very aware of Billy's closeness; they were almost chest-to-chest. "Yeah, to a bar where I could blend in with the crowd, not a party with gorgeous people. I'll stick out like a sore thumb."

"You're going."

Jordan laughed. "No, I'm not."

Billy narrowed his eyes. "I'll blow you."

Jordan was set to call Billy's bluff. "Yeah? Payment up front."

There was a moment of sexual tension between them. Billy puckered his lips, blew a stream of air at Jordan, and said, "There, I blew you. You're going."

"You're not funny," Jordan growled.

Billy grinned triumphantly. "I'm hilarious and you know it. Now, go post your script."

"Fuck you." Jordan stormed to the couch.

"If you're good."

The playful argument continued the next day in the changing room of the retail store.

"No, no, no, no!" Jordan shoved Billy out of the changing room with an armful of clothes. "No to trying on those clothes! No to you being in here while I change! No to going to the party!" Jordan shut the door on Billy.

He didn't like the smug tone in Billy's voice when he said, "Fine. Get dressed."

Jordan looked around the changing room. He closed his eyes. "Billy, where are my *actual* clothes?"

"Out here with me, and you'll only get them back once you try on the other ones. Don't forget to work that catwalk for me with every outfit." Billy tossed some of the clothes over the changing room door.

"I hate you." Jordan pouted back.

Billy laughed. "You love me. Now, get dressed and show me that walk."

Friday night, they were both a bundle of nerves. The moment Jordan clocked out, Billy handed him a vodka shot, then rushed him to eat. "Drake and Derek will be here at nine," Billy reminded him. "I can't believe we're going to a Lexi Luscious party. Make sure you talk to everyone you can. You never know who can help you in your writing career."

Before Jordan chewed his final bite, Billy whisked away his plate, replacing it with a cocktail. "Pregame, to settle our nerves," Billy said, holding out his own glass in a toast. "To the opportunities before us!"

"To the opportunities before us," Jordan returned. He took a sip, then nearly gagged at the potency. "My God, is there any mixer in this?!"

Billy took another long gulp. "A little. Now, go shower."

Jordan took another sip, this one going down slightly easier than the first. "This is important to you, isn't it?"

Billy took another healthy drink and replied, "It's like my official debut here." Billy paused. Glowering at him, he ordered, "Shower. Now."

Jordan got up, drink in hand. He pointed his drink at Billy, "I'm going, and no trying to help me. I mean it."

Two hours later, they arrived in the car Drake and Derek hired for the night. Jordan slowed Billy down in drinking, making him down two bottles of water before their arrival. The closer they were to the party, the less jittery Billy became. The mask Jordan saw at the shoot slowly crept over Billy's face.

The party was just as over-the-top as Jordan expected. Colorful lights flashed all around the California home in the hills. There was a DJ in the main room spinning music, several open bars with scantily clad bartenders to suit everyone's tastes. What intimidated Jordan the most was all the beautiful people milling about.

The party was filled with top adult film stars, social media influencers, reality stars, people whose claim to fame was they simply existed, and other people who made sure that everyone knew them. Looking around, the feeling of not belonging hit Jordan square in the face.

Drake clasped Jordan's shoulder and said, "Let's get our boys some drinks, shall we?"

Jordan looked to Billy who smiled and nodded. "Okay."

Jordan let Drake peel him away from the group; he had never felt more uncomfortable in his skin even though people smiled and greeted them as they made their way to the nearest bar.

Drake turned to Jordan while they waited for their drinks, told him to relax, and massaged Jordan's shoulder. "These are just people like you. At one time or another, they were struggling to make it in this business."

Jordan shook his head and countered, "These people are nothing like me. I shouldn't have come. I'm going to fuck this all up for Billy, I just know it."

The shirtless bartender in skin-tight trunks placed their drinks in front of them. "You're not going to do anything of the sort," Drake said, picking up their drinks, "and Billy wanted you here, and you want to be here for Billy. Just relax and have fun. Tell people about that funny script on your site."

Jordan took a sip of his drink. "Okay. Wait… what funny script on my site?"

Drake chuckled. "The one about the diva porn star. I sent it to everyone I know. You should see about making it a short film." Drake motioned out to the crowd with the hand clutching his drink. "Out there is the person or people who can make it happen. Network."

Jordan tried. For the most part, he hung in Billy's shadow as they made their way through the party. Billy was met warmly, and people asked him to collaborate in filming content, but Jordan was ignored seemingly right after they discovered he was a writer. No matter how Billy tried to steer the conversation to Jordan, they veered right back to Billy.

"I'll go get us some fresh drinks," Jordan told Billy, needing to extricate himself from being ignored in the crowd.

Jordan parked himself at the bar, waiting for the bartenders to notice him among the sea of beautiful people. "Not having a good time?" Jordan turned to see a slender woman in a modest, skin-tight blue dress with hair the color of straw curling around a warm, bright face that made him instantly like her.

Jordan gave her a weak smile and confided, "I'm here for a friend. I'm not pretty or talented enough to be one of these people. Hell, I can barely get a drink here."

Concern etched across the woman's face. "Why do you say that?"

Jordan shrugged. "Every time I tell someone I'm a writer, they instantly shut down. It's okay. Like I said, I'm really here for my friend, Billy."

The woman extended a perfectly manicured hand to Jordan. "What is your name?"

Jordan took her hand. "Jordan. Jordan Hudson."

Her face went from concern to puzzlement as she said, "I know that name. Where do I know that name from?" She withdrew her hand and pulled out her phone.

"You really shouldn't know me." Jordan laughed.

She looked up at him with what mirrored a disapproving mother's glare but kept her ultra-red lips smiling. "I do, and you should check your DMs more often you do, naughty boy."

Jordan grabbed his phone. "Shit. I turned the notifications off and forgot to put them back on after that first post with Billy. I really haven't looked at my Twitter since." Jordan now saw he had more than ninety-nine notifications of likes, comments, and retweets. He also had a few messages waiting for him. "Shit, that's a lot of notifications." He looked up at the women with a grimace. "Language. Sorry."

She waved over a bartender. "Don't be sorry—just check your messages. Get me and this man a drink and a shot." When the bartender returned, she leaned over the counter and pointedly told him, "Make sure he gets served quickly from now on. He's my special guest."

Jordan read and reread the message from Lexi Luscious. *I loved your script, Porn Diva. I'd like to talk to you about it. I'm having a party this Friday. I would love for you to come.*

Jordan looked up, dumbfounded. The woman held out a shot for him as he told her, "Lexi Luscious wants to meet me."

She smiled at him. "Yes, yes, I do. Now are you going to take this shot with me or not?"

Jordan took the shot from Lexi. Then, it hit him. "Oh, my God. I can't believe I didn't recognize you. I'm so sorry."

"Just be sorry you're making me wait to take this shot. Cheers!" They clinked shot glasses and downed the colorful liquid. "We'll talk business later. Who did you say you were here with?"

Jordan coughed from the burn of alcohol but managed, "Billy. Billy Chase. He's over there."

Lexi made a sound of disgust. "It looks like my nephew's fiancé, Alex, is headed his way. You better go rescue him." She handed Jordan his drink. "Don't forget to check your DMs."

Jordan took the drink and pulled out his phone for show. "I will. I promise. Thank you so much!" Against his better judgment, he hugged her and said, "Thank you. Thank you. Thank you."

Lexi laughed, patting him on the back. "You're welcome. Now, go rescue your boyfriend."

Jordan let go. "We're just friends, but you really don't care about that." Jordan hugged her one more time, then rushed off to Billy.

He opened up his phone and went through the other messages. Jordan stopped. The smile on his face quickly wilted. He nearly dropped his drink when he read the oldest message and prayed it wasn't true. *Oh, my God. Billy.*

FIGHTS AND FLIGHTS

BILLY WAS ENJOYING himself. He was making connections, getting his name out "there," and hopefully finding more work. Hunter gave him those three shoots, but now he was on his own. He tried to get people talking to Jordan, but no matter how hard he tried, they ignored him the moment they heard Jordan was a writer.

When Jordan begged off to get another drink, Billy didn't want to let him go. He wanted to grab Jordan by the hand and make him stay right there. He wanted to tell all of them they were idiots for treating Jordan the way they had, that one day he'd throw parties like this they would die to attend.

The latest people to snub Jordan had moved on, leaving Billy to wait for Jordan's return. He looked back into the house and saw Jordan at the bar talking to someone. *Finally, he's making connections.* Billy smiled. He turned around to scan for anyone he hadn't talked to and should. That's when he spotted Alex and his crew heading right toward him. *Fuck.*

"Billy, do you know a Kevin from some old site called Country Boyz?" He turned to see Jordan's concerned face. "Billy, do you know him?"

He exhaled the tension from his body. Having Jordan there calmed him. "Yeah, that was the site that started my porn career. Why do you ask?" He saw the concern in Jordan's eyes.

"Billy, I think you should sit down. I have something to tell you." Jordan's voice was soft but instant.

Flippant, Billy said, "Just tell me."

"Billy, that was pretty shitty what you did to Dennis and me," a voice said from behind Billy.

Billy rolled his eyes before turning to see the man that called his name. Plastering on a fake smile and he said, "Alex, so good to see you here. Which one of these three is your actual fiancé and which two are your side pieces?"

If the men were bothered by the comment, they didn't show it. "You should have kept your nose out of our business. Maybe if you had, he wouldn't have been kidnapped."

That hurt Billy. Since it happened, he blamed himself. "Or it would have happened sooner when his heart broke because he found out you got married."

"Billy, we seriously need to talk," Jordan insisted as he pulled on his arm.

The young twink-ish brunette in the middle crossed his arms and glowered at Alex. "What is he talking about? Why would you have broken Dennis's

heart? You said Billy bad-mouthed you to Dennis and Hunter. That's why you can't film with them anymore."

Billy's grin was all teeth and full of bite as he replied, "Your fiancé doesn't know you tried to turn your twosome into a threesome?"

Alex sputtered at his fiancé, "He did… sort of. It doesn't matter. He just ruined things between Dennis and me. I'll explain later, Cameron."

Jordan pulled on his arm again, more insistently this time. "Billy, seriously, we need to talk. I have something important to tell you."

Alex directed his attack at Jordan. "Who's this? Your *boyfriend*? Didn't know you were a chubby-chaser."

"Billy, is everything okay over here?" Derek asked, walking up with Drake.

Alex's fiancé knocked his hand off him, exclaiming, "You fucking slut! I told you I didn't want to have an open relationship outside of your work."

Jordan tugged again. "Billy, *please*."

Alex continued his attack at Jordan and spat, "I think your boyfriend's hungry. Better go slop your hog."

Multiple hands held Billy back from attacking Alex. "He's not my boyfriend, but I'd be damn lucky if he was. He's sweet and kind and doesn't judge people like *you*. I'd date him in a heartbeat."

The crowd parted for Lexi to address the scene. "Is everything okay here, gentlemen?" eyeing each of them, reading the situation. "Cameron?"

"It's nothing, Lexi," Alex answered, glaring at Billy.

She cocked her head at Alex. "I believe I was asking Cameron."

The young man looked to Billy, then to Alex. He ground his teeth in contemplation and resigned, "No, it's not." He pulled the ring off his finger and dropped it onto the ground. "My ex-fiancé was just leaving. Have your shit out of my condo by Monday." With that, Cameron turned and left.

"Cameron!" Alex called out. He turned back to Billy and threatened, "You'll pay for this." Picking the ring off the ground, he chased after Cameron.

The hands released Billy. "I'm so sorry, Lexi," he said.

She held up a hand for him to stop talking. "I can't stand that arrogant fuck. You did me a favor." Then, her eyes went to Jordan, and she said, "Actually, you did me two. You brought this little gem with you."

Billy turned around to face Jordan. Jordan said, "Billy, we need to talk."

"I know, that whole I-would-date-you thing." Billy ran his hand over his hair. "I know it just sort of came out, but I meant it."

Jordan put his hand over Billy's mouth to get him to stop talking. "Will you shut up and let me talk?!" Jordan removed his hand when Billy nodded. "Your friend Kevin sent me a message in hopes of contacting you." Jordan took in a deep breath. "It's your mother. She's in the hospital. He said she was in an accident."

The next hours were a blur for Billy. He remembered collapsing, people picking him up, carrying him inside, talking both to and at him. He stared, glassy-eyed, nodding and giving one-word answers. Next, he was back in the same car in which they arrived. Jordan

153

had gotten out at some point, and he was gone for a long time.

Billy heard the trunk close. Jordan was back, and the car began moving again. This time when it stopped, Billy left the car with Jordan; they were at the airport. Jordan grabbed two bags from the trunk. Billy was pulled into the airport. They went through line after line before they sat on hard chairs.

Jordan pulled him to his feet and walked him down the gate to a plane. Jordan put him in his seat. He put away the bags and sat beside Billy. Jordan's hands fastened the seatbelt around his lap. More people got on. The plane's engines turned on. A safety video played in front of Billy.

The engines roared to life, and Jordan took his hand. Billy squeezed it, needing to know Jordan was there beside him. The plane started moving. He closed his eyes. He felt the pressure of the plane speeding across the runway and jumping into the air. The pilot said something over the speakers that he didn't hear.

Turning his head and opening his eyes, he saw Jordan watching him. He squeezed Jordan's hand and said, "I'm going to sleep now. Thank you."

Jordan stroked Billy's face with his other hand. Jordan kissed Billy on the cheek. "I should be thanking you. Let's try to get some sleep, okay?"

Billy reclined his seat. "Jordan? It's going to be okay, right?"

"Yes, Billy. Everything is going to be okay," Jordan lied.

21

RETURN TO THE CANDY SHOP

CRYING INTO HIS gag, Kevin fruitlessly pulled at the zip ties that bound his wrists behind his back. He was naked and on a filthy mattress in what were the remains of a Candy Shop. He only knew this from the flashes of a vague, drug-fueled haze in his memory. He never should have gotten in that car, never should have let that man drive him away from the underpass he called home that night.

The promise of fifty bucks and the lure of the little baggy filled with meth and a pipe was too much for Kevin. His skin crawled with the need for another hit. Begging on street corners by day and trying to sell his emaciated body and useless cock hadn't earned him much the past few days. People were growing numb to his presence and ungracious in his inability to perform.

When the slick black SUV stopped under the bridge, he crept down from the shadows. The tinted window of the passenger door rolled down when he was just a foot away. Despite it being nearly midnight, the man inside wore mirrored sunglasses, a hat with the brim pulled low, and collar flipped up. The sneer he gave Kevin should have sent him scurrying away, but Kevin was enticed by the treats in the baggy dangling from the man's hand. Kevin licked his lips.

Kevin didn't see the man's mouth move when he spoke, "This and fifty bucks for a good time. You getting in or what?"

"Yeah," Kevin agreed as he opened the passenger door, eyes on his prize. He tried to snatch the baggy from the man as he got in, but the man pulled it out of his reach. "Come on, man. Just a taste to tide me over."

The man pressed a button on his driver's side door and rolled up the passenger window. Putting the SUV in drive, he said, "You can have all you want when we get to where we're going."

Buckling his seatbelt, Kevin chose to sit in the back seat. He tried not to scratch at his skin. His body shivered with the need for more poison. The man didn't say anything to him, didn't even look at him while they drove into the outskirts of town. Kevin didn't recognize the route they were going until they arrived at the now defunct Candy Shop.

"Do you bring all your tricks to such nice places?" Kevin had joked, absentmindedly scratching at his neck.

The man handed Kevin the baggy and a lighter. "Smoke it outside. I don't want my car smelling of that shit."

Kevin took his prize and got out. With shaking hands, he carefully pulled out the pipe. He almost lost

the precious crystal with his twitching hand, but he successfully got it out of the baggy and into the pipe. Raising the clear glass pipe to his lips, he flicked the lighter and heated the glass underneath to liquidate the precious toxin.

The putrid smoke filled his lungs. Kevin's mind calmed and the itching seemed to fade away. Pulling the pipe away, Kevin held onto the venomous smoke for as long he could, then exhaled it into the night. He repeated it over and over again until the translucent rock was a black residue.

Kevin hadn't heard the man get out and come around the vehicle. He took the pipe from him and put another rock in it. "Smoke it all. I don't have any use for it, and I got more for later."

Kevin gave the man his ragged smile and said, "Thanks." The man watched him smoke. High, Kevin stumbled a bit when he tried to lower the pipe, but the man grabbed him by the wrist and brought the pipe back up until he smoked all of it. "I, uh, think I'm good for a bit."

He fell down onto the ground in a euphoric bliss. Spreading himself out on the dirt and grass, he smiled. "There you are," he said to no one. "How I missed you." He felt himself rising. "Whoa, I'm flying." He moved his arms wildly about. "Weeeee!" He was moving in the air.

He suddenly fell from the sky, but landed on a hard, yet fluffy cloud. "Fuck." He felt hands on him, tugging his clothes off... He remembered the man. "You want to have some fun now, big boy?" His shirt came off,

followed by his pants and dirty underwear. "I'm a real good time. I used to do porn. Did you know that?"

The man said nothing. He rolled Kevin onto his stomach, took his roaming arms, and pinned them to the small of his back. "Hey, not so rough," Kevin giggled. Something was slipped around his wrists and pulled tight. "What are you doing?" The man did the same thing to his ankles. "You like it kinky, huh?" A leather gag wrapped around his head and silenced Kevin.

The man walked away, leaving Kevin helpless on the mattress in the abandoned building. Kevin rolled himself over and laughed into the gag. *I bet he's going to get his buddies.* Kevin had done this before, letting the good old boys that like to teach fags like him a lesson by showing them how real men fucked.

He closed his eyes. *I'll just sleep until they get here.* No one came. When Kevin woke up, he didn't have leaking cum from the sore ass he was expecting. He struggled against his bonds. He needed something to drink. He needed to piss. He needed another hit. He screamed into the leather gag.

His bladder emptied several times all over himself. The stench from soiling himself while he slept off his high rankled his nose. In nothing but darkness, Kevin didn't know if he'd been there a few hours or a few days. He had all but given up hope when he heard the crunch of footsteps on the remains of the shop floor.

A light cut through the darkness and into his eyes. He turned his head away from the searing pain of it. He screamed for help into the gag and turned his head back into the light. It was the man who brought him here. Kevin's pleas to be released were unintelligible through the leather gag.

The man crouched down. Setting the light down on the floor, he pulled a small black satchel from behind him. "Fucking junkies. That amount of meth should have killed you." The man pulled a needle from the satchel and removed the safety tip. Plunging it into Kevin's arm, he said, "That's enough to kill a horse. If you survive that, you deserve to live."

Kevin's muffled screams faded with the flow of liquid death in his veins. A calming fog misted over his consciousness. He lost feeling in the arm first, then it spread throughout his body. His heart raced wildly, threatening to crack open his chest. His eyes grew heavy. *I'll just take a little nap.* Kevin's eyes closed. *A little nap.*

GOING HOME

"**ARE YOU SURE** you called every hospital? What did the message say exactly?" Billy asked, speeding down the highway. The closest airport was an hour away from where Billy grew up.

Jordan switched back to his Twitter and read the message aloud. "Hey, do you know Billy Chase? I saw you in a few of his posts. Can you please tell him to come home quick? His mom was in a horrible accident. It's really bad. Tell him I'm Kevin from Country Boyz." Jordan put the phone down. "I tried messaging the account back, but it's been deactivated."

Billy's knuckles went white from gripping the steering wheel so tight. "Kevin from Country Boyz? He didn't know my mother. Let me see the message."

"Not while you're driving and…" Jordan leaned over and checked the speedometer, "not while you're doing ninety miles an hour."

Billy slowed down to eighty. "What do you think we should do?"

Jordan shrugged. "Let's go to your mom's house. Maybe one of her neighbors knows something."

Billy muttered under his breath. "Or the latest leech on her couch does. Guess I'm going home."

Thirty minutes later, Billy slowed the rental car to a stop in front of his childhood home. It was just as he remembered it, broken and run-down. A newer car sat in the driveway. The lawn looked freshly cut. Turning the engine off, he looked to Jordan who pat his knee, and then they got out. Billy took a few deep breaths and made his way up to the front door, Jordan at his side.

He didn't expect anyone to answer when he rang the bell. The woman who answered certainly didn't expect him or his exclamation of, "What the fuck?"

The woman squinted and opened the door. "Billy? Is that you? What are you doing here?"

Jordan caught Billy before he crumbled to the floor. He lifted Billy back to his feet. "Hi, ma'am, um Ms. Chase. We were told you were in a horrible accident. Obviously, that's not the case."

The woman quirked an eyebrow at them. "Billy, are you spinning tall tales again?" Ms. Chase looked about. "Come on in before you have the whole neighborhood gossiping."

They followed Ms. Chase into the house. The house wasn't as Billy remembered it. The couch Bobby Lee normally resided on was gone, replaced with a new model with far less stains. There were crosses and pictures of Jesus on the wall where his school pictures once hung.

161

Sitting on the couch beside his mother, Billy commented, "You redecorated. What does Bobby Lee think of it?'

Ms. Chase eyed Jordan sitting on the couch's matching chair. "I threw that loser out a long, long time ago." She refocused her attention on Billy. "He didn't like that I found the church."

Billy closed his eyes and raised a finger asking, "Wait. If he's been gone all this time, why haven't you tried to get in touch with me? Why haven't you answered any of my calls or texts? You could cash those checks I sent, but not pick up the phone to talk to your son?"

"Billy, that's family business. We shouldn't discuss that in front of others." Ms. Chase chuckled nervously, patting Billy on the knee.

"He is family." Billy looked at Jordan, then looked back at his mother. "He's my boyfriend."

Jordan stood, flustered. "Why don't I go get us something to eat? Billy and I haven't eaten since last night. I thought I saw some sort of burger joint down the street. What would you like, Ms. Chase?"

"Bless your heart. A cheeseburger and fries would be lovely," she answered, with false sweetness. "Oh, and a sweet tea. I don't suppose you know anything about sweet tea out West?"

Jordan took the keys from Billy. "Yes, ma'am. Billy makes it for me all the time." Jordan thought he saw her shudder at his comment but continued, "I'll be right back in a bit."

Ms. Chase waited until Jordan was gone before she continued, "There, now that we're alone… Baby,

how are you? Are you ready to stop that whole gay thing yet?"

Billy looked at his mother as if she were a stranger. "Is me being gay a problem for you? You never had a problem with it before."

She patted his knee again. "Love the sinner, not the sin."

Billy recoiled from her touch. "What's going on here? You found religion. I get it. Good for you, but I just flew across the country for you, thanks to the man to whom you were just Southern-rude."

Ms. Chase's gaze grew stern. "Billy, I was not rude, and I will not be talked to like that in my house by some filthy, gay, porn person. Your friend Teddy was right. You haven't changed."

Billy stood, not believing what he was hearing. "Not rude? Everyone knows 'bless your heart' is Southern for 'fuck you!'"

"Billy! Language!" Ms. Chase scolded sharply.

Billy continued unabated, "How do you know Teddy anyway? I haven't talked to him since you threw me out of your home. By the way, that was very *Christian* of you."

A knock at the door broke Billy's tirade. "Calm yourself," Ms. Chase ordered, getting up. "I don't need the whole neighborhood knowing my business." When his mother opened the door, Billy couldn't believe who it was. He was a little thicker, a little older, but it was him. "Hello, Teddy."

Teddy gave her a courtesy nod. "Hello, Ms. Chase." He looked past her to Billy and said, "Hello, Billy. I heard you were back in town."

Billy was taken back to a time when he and Teddy were more than friends. "What are you doing here?"

Teddy gave Billy that lopsided, scoundrel smile. "To see you, of course. Ms. Chase, if it wouldn't be too much to ask, could I steal Billy for a little bit? I would love to catch up with him."

Smiling brightly at Teddy, Ms. Chase said, "Not at all. He needs to cool off. Go on, Billy. Go catch up with Teddy. I'll tell your friend you'll be back shortly."

Billy took one step, then rushed Teddy. Hugging him close, Billy almost cried. "I've missed you."

Teddy laughed. "I missed you too, Billy. Come on, let's go for a walk."

"Okay, how did you know I was in town?" Billy followed Teddy out the door. Billy jumped with the *thwack* of the closing screen door.

Teddy kept walking toward the back of the house. "A famous porn star like you doesn't come to town without the whole town knowing." Teddy turned around to look at Billy and continued, "I was up the street when your mother texted me two strange men were at her door."

Billy caught up to Teddy. He recognized where they were headed. "That's nice of you to keep an eye on my mother. A walk through the woods and memory lane?"

Teddy bumped Billy's shoulder. "Something like that. Figured you'd like to see it."

"I guess." The shade of the trees started covering them as they stepped onto the overgrown path. "What is your wife going to say about you hanging around me? Did you guys have a boy or a girl?" Billy ventured.

"Not married. No kid either," Teddy answered, stomping through the woods.

"What happened?"

There was a bit of bitterness in Teddy's voice when he said, "I'll tell you when we get to the clearing."

"Okay." Billy said nothing more as he swatted mosquitos and prayed nothing more was going to jump out and bite him. A few minutes later, they broke through the undergrowth of the woods to the clearing. "It's just like I remember." Billy laughed as he pushed past Teddy to twirl around in the sun. "We did so many naughty things here."

Billy stopped when he got dizzy. He looked at Teddy with a puzzled expression. Teddy was down on one knee, messing with his pants leg. "Something bite you?"

Teddy rose, pointing the small gun at Billy. "Nope. You ruined my life, Billy. And for that, you're going to die."

TWO BLUE-HAIRED LADIES

JORDAN DIDN'T LIKE the look of the man staring at him from the SUV, scowling, across the street from where they parked the rental. He chalked it up to the small mindedness of a Southern rural town. Getting in the car, he noticed in the rearview mirror the man was watching him with unhealthy interest.

Starting the engine, Jordan pulled out into the road, hoping the man wouldn't follow him. He knew that look; it was the look of hate and disgust. It was the look of false Christians who shouted that you were going to Hell, or the look of men on the cusp of unceasingly punching you until you drew your last breath.

When he saw the man wasn't following him, Jordan let out the breath he had been holding since he first saw him. Turning at the end of the street, and again at the next street over, Jordan drove back to the local fast-food joint. The drive-through was three cars deep, but he noticed the lobby was virtually empty.

Taking a chance, he parked the car and headed inside. There were three people ahead of him. Behind the counter stood a young woman with curly black hair pulled into a tight ponytail who popped her gum. She waited for the man ordering to decide what he wanted. Jordan would have gone back to his car and tried his luck in the drive thru, but the two blue-haired old women gossiping caught his attention.

"If you tell me, Mable, that man is murdering all the right people. I don't see why they're trying to catch him. He's doing this country a great service."

Mable smacked the other woman's hand. "Ethel, I can't believe you would say that," and shook her head in sorrow. "I can't imagine what that poor family is going through. First, someone plasters his naughty bits all over the town to see, then his parents find him floating in the lake. Then, they had to watch that video of him getting murdered."

Ethel raised her left hand up in the air. "Thank God for cameras. I have them all over my house, you know. Of course, it was cameras that got those boys wrong with God. Imagine filming yourself doing *that*. In our day, we kept it private and in the bedroom."

Mable side-bumped her friend. "Oh, Ethel, get with the times. In our day it would have taken too long to paint it on the cave walls." Both women laughed at their joke. "I wonder if they are going to find those other two boys from that boy country site."

"Excuse me, ladies. I didn't mean to eavesdrop." Both women turned to look at Jordan.

Ethel scowled at him. "Then don't."

Jordan gave a conciliatory nod. "Yes, ma'am. I know, but the damage is done. You wouldn't be talking about the Country Boyz site, would you?"

Mable tapped Ethel on the shoulder. "That's the name of it. Country Boyz, with a z." Mable eyed Jordan with a little more interest than what was comfortable. "You're not one of those porn people, are you?"

Jordan laughed. "Me? No, I mean look at me."

Ethel looked him up and down. "Some of us like a man with some meat on his bones."

Jordan felt his cheeks flush red with embarrassment, but he stayed on task. "Thank you. What's going on with the Country Boyz?" He then clarified, "I'm not from around here, and I just got into town."

Mable lowered her voice as if she was sharing something that shouldn't be overheard, "Someone is going around killing them. They got four that we know of so far. They are looking for the other two now to get them in police protection."

"All they know is it's someone dressed all in black and drives a black SUV," Ethel added, proud she could add that tiny bit. "They caught it on camera when he killed that poor Henderson boy."

Pieces started clicking into place for Jordan. "No." He stepped back. The two women looked at him confused. "No, no, no." Jordan ran out of the restaurant and jumped back into the car. He pulled out his phone and called 9-1-1. The tires screeched as he pulled out of the space and into the road, jumping the curb.

"9-1-1, what's the nature of your emergency?" answered the almost-chipper voice.

Jordan rattled off Ms. Chase's address and demanded they send the police, S.W.A.T, the National Guard, and anyone else with a badge. "Someone is trying to kill my friend!" Jordan saw Billy walking around the house with the man from the SUV. "Shit. Hurry!"

Jordan slammed on the brakes in front of Ms. Chase's house. He threw the car in park and jumped out, not bothering to turn the engine off. Ms. Chase came out when she saw him. "Leave him alone, you queer. He's catching up with his friend." Jordan ignored her. "Are you just going to leave that hunk of junk running in my yard?"

Jordan rushed to the back. He looked around to see where they had gone. He thought he saw a flash of Billy's blue shirt in the woods. *I hope this is the right way,* Jordan thought, stumbling through the trail. He was relieved and terrified when he heard the crunch of leaves and twigs ahead of him. *Please be wrong. Please be wrong.*

Jordan stopped when he saw the back of the man he assumed was from the SUV. Billy was in a clearing, his hands raised. The man from the SUV had his arm raised, gun pointing at Billy. "You ruined my life, Billy." Jordan heard the man say as he inched closer. "For that, you're going to die."

BECAUSE OF YOU

RAISING HIS HANDS in a placating manner, Billy asked, "How did I ruin your life? I mean, I left town. I haven't seen you in years."

Teddy's eyes grew wide with rage. He waved the gun around recklessly. "Really, Billy? Really? Everything in my life turned to shit, and it was because of you!"

Billy darted his eyes back and forth. "I'm sorry for what you think I did?"

"Is that a fucking question?" Teddy's body began to shake with fury at Billy's indignation.

Billy began slowly backing away, saying, "I'm sorry. I don't know what I did to ruin your life."

Teddy cocked his head to the side. Billy's heart leaped into this throat when he caught a glimpse of Jordan behind him. "What you did? What you did?! I'll tell you what you did. You sucked my dick and turned me gay, for one."

"You know that's not how it works. You're either gay, or you're not." Billy inched back a little farther.

"Stop trying to get away!" Billy froze. "You're going to hear everything you did to me, and then I'm going to shoot you. Then, I'm going to go back to your mama's house and shoot her bitchy-ass and that faggot boyfriend of yours."

Billy saw Jordan scrounging around in the woods behind Teddy. "Leave them out of this. It's between you and me. Go on—tell me what I did."

Teddy wiped the sweat from his brow with his other arm, then reiterated, "You sucked my dick and turned me gay. Then, when Debra came saying she was pregnant, my father told me I had to marry the bitch. What was I going to do? Tell my dad I never stuck my dick in her stank pussy because I was sticking it up your ass?"

"You never slept with her? Then why did you marry her?" Billy wanted to hug Teddy.

Teddy started waving the gun around again and said, "I didn't. My mom must have sensed something was up because she kept pushing the wedding back and back until that baby came out." Teddy narrowed his eyes at Billy. "The baby came out black. Black! It was a fucking n–"

"Don't you dare finish that sentence," Billy warned. He shook his head slightly at Jordan who had found a small branch and was brandishing it like a club behind Teddy. "How is that *my* fault?"

Teddy sneered at Billy. "Had you stayed, or fought harder for me to go with you, I wouldn't have had to give up my scholarship and start working in that

171

shithole warehouse where Dad got me a job because I had to provide for my family."

"You sent *me* away, Teddy."

Teddy shouted back, spittle spraying from his mouth, "You should have fought harder!"

Billy moved his raised palms back and forth. "Okay, okay. You're right. I should have fought harder. What else?"

Billy saw the madness in Teddy's eyes. "What else?! What else?! Of course, I thought I was in love with you. I went looking for you. Heard you were staying at some old fag's house out in the country." Teddy's nostrils flared. "I went there looking for you, but you'd already moved on. That's what you do, isn't it, Billy? Move on?"

Billy swallowed hard. He saw Jordan holding onto a branch with two hands and resting it on his shoulder moving slowly behind Teddy. "No! I mean yes. That's what I do."

Teddy let out a blood-curdling laugh, the mania spreading through him. "You were gone, but your little buddy Brett asked if I'd like fuck on camera." Billy took a calming breath. "I was horny and missing you, so I said, 'what the Hell?' It was a one-time thing, and I needed the money. No one I knew was going to see it anyways, right?" Teddy punched the gun at Billy. "Right?!"

Billy watched Jordan cautiously getting closer to Teddy. "Right... someone you know saw it, didn't they?"

Teddy pressed the gun to his head, then yanked it away when he yelled, "Bingo!" He pointed it back at

Billy. "Ask me how I know he saw it?" The frenzied smile on Teddy's face filled Billy with fear. "I'll tell you. My dad saw it. Do you know how I know?" Billy felt the fear in the pit of his stomach. "We were out in the bay, fishing in his boat. Normal Saturday. We had a few beers. Then he looked at me and said, 'I saw that video you did. So, you're a fag.'"

Billy watched Jordan pause when Teddy started hitting his head with the side of the pistol. "He said, 'Since you like sucking dick, how about you do your dad a favor?'" Billy's jaw dropped. "He pulled out his dick and tried to get me to suck him." Teddy shook his head in disbelief. "He had a heart attack while I was trying to fight him off. Out on the water."

"I'm so sorry."

Teddy punched the gun at Billy again. "Don't be! I sat there and finished my beer while he died." Teddy let out another maniacal laugh. "Of course, the fuck had us in hock up to our eyeballs. We lost the house. My mother and sisters had to move in with my grandparents. Me? Me? I was on my own. I wouldn't have made that video. My dad wouldn't have seen it if I wasn't looking for you."

"I, uh… didn't mean to." Billy tried to wave Jordan away without drawing Teddy's attention.

Teddy mocked, "I didn't mean to. I busted my ass at that warehouse, but it wasn't enough. Then I happened to stop at a gas station, and who do you think I saw?"

"I don't know."

173

Teddy scoffed. "Your buddy, Brett. He didn't even recognize me. He ruined my life, and he didn't even recognize me!"

"W-what did you do?" Billy saw Jordan too close for his own comfort.

"I fucked him." Teddy shrugged. "That wasn't enough, though. I wanted my revenge. I needed my revenge for what they did. They had to pay. You had to pay. You all had to pay." A sinister grin spread across Teddy's face as he continued, "First, I pushed that old fuck down the stairs. That was easy."

Billy covered his mouth with one hand and said, "Joe."

Teddy laughed. "The Asian guy, I burned him alive in his own home. Of course, if he had the good sense to die when I ran him and his boyfriend off the road, I wouldn't have had to. I got tired of seeing them flaunting the happiness I couldn't have!"

"Mario and Randy."

"I was saving Brett for last, but the dumb fuck had to go and check in on that old fuck." Billy hated the pleasure in Teddy's voice as he spoke, "I just let myself in his trailer, blew out the pilot light, and turned on all the burners on the stove." Teddy cackled. "He never woke up."

Billy was near tears now.

"I decided to play with the uppity, straight boy." Billy couldn't understand the evil in Teddy; this wasn't the Teddy he knew. "I sent everyone *he* knew pictures of him in action on that piece-of-shit site."

Billy wiped the tears from his eyes. He didn't want to know, but he still asked, "What did you do to Keith?"

"I waited until he was broken and ruined. When he was drunk, I smashed his head with a baseball bat and tossed him into the lake to drown." Billy cringed at the joy Teddy had at recounting his exploits. "That one he used to fuck, his fag buddy? He wasn't a challenge at all. Ending him was an act of kindness."

"Kevin," Billy choked on a sob.

"I picked his drug-addicted ass up under a freeway, took him to that abandoned bar, the Candy Shop, you used to frequent, and pumped him full of drugs until his heart stopped. Fucking waste of time, but I had to make him pay, just like the others." Teddy sneered in disgust.

"Shadow?" Billy asked, not wanting to hear anymore, but he needing to know.

"Oh, I haven't found him yet… but I will." Teddy's face lit up with delight.

Jordan was almost on Teddy now. Billy wanted to scream for him to run, not be an idiot, and go get help, but he couldn't risk Teddy turning the gun on him. "Teddy, you don't have to do this. Turn yourself in, and we can get you help."

"You think I need help? You're the sick fuck who needs help. Putting your ass on display for all those perverts." Billy cringed when Jordan accidently snapped a twig. Teddy turned and pointed the gun at the approaching Jordan.

He waved the gun exclaiming, "Look what we have here! Someone's trying to be a hero. Drop it and put your hands up." Terror griped Billy when Teddy added, "I think I'll kill you right now, so Billy can watch."

"Why, Jordan?" Billy had tears streaming down his face.

"I couldn't let him hurt you," Jordan confessed, still brandishing the branch.

"Put the branch down," Teddy ordered.

Jordan looked at Billy. Billy shook his head 'no.' Jordan looked back at Teddy. "You want me to put this branch down? Fine. Here."

Jordan sent the branch flying up in the air at Teddy, and Teddy instinctively covered his face with his arms to protect himself. Jordan ran at Teddy, crashing into his middle. Billy, not even realizing he was doing it, ran at Teddy and tackled his legs out from under him. Teddy pulled the trigger, sending a bullet flying before he landed roughly, his head bouncing on the ground. The gun fired again before Teddy lost his grip on it.

"Get the gun!" Jordan shouted, his ears ringing from the shots. Billy and Jordan scrambled to find the gun while Teddy tried to regain his senses. They saw movement in the wood. "Over here!" Jordan shouted as he saw Teddy begin to get up. "Oh, no you don't, you sick fuck," and Jordan dropped his full body weight onto Teddy's chest, knocking the air from his lungs.

"I got the gun!" Billy announced loudly, holding the offending weapon by two fingers.

Uniformed cops came crashing through the under-brush of the woods pointing their guns at all of them. "Freeze! Drop the gun!"

"What? I'm just going to put this down here, okay?" Billy shouted back, the ringing in his ears too loud for him to understand them.

Puzzled by Billy's response, the uniformed cops looked at each other. One of them started talking into the radio on his shoulder while the other cautiously moved to the place Billy put down the gun and kicked it away from him. They saw more uniforms coming through the woods. Billy had his arm twisted behind his back and cuffs snapped around his wrist. He watched another officer do the same to Jordan and Teddy.

Billy shouted, annoyed. "Hey! We're the victims here!"

EPILOGUE

"**O**KAY, PEOPLE. PLACES!** Let's try to get this in one take!" Lexi shouted to the crew.

Jordan thought he was dreaming. He had put in notice at his customer service job and was now working for Lexi full-time. "I can't believe we're shooting this."

"Believe it. It's fantastic, Mr. Writer. You wrote it, and your sexy boyfriend is starring in it. My first non-sex role!" Billy exclaimed as Jordan pulled the makeup bib off his neck.

Jordan straightened Billy's shirt. "And I told you you're an actor. I just can't get over the fact that you're my boyfriend. Like, I get to *actually* sleep with you."

Billy put a hand on Jordan's shoulder. "Believe it, and it's *me* who gets to sleep with *you*."

Jordan laughed at Billy's wiggling eyebrows. "Remember we have to pack when we get home. We have an early morning flight."

Billy groaned. "How many times are they going to question us? We've given our statements. He confessed. Cut-and-dry."

Jordan grew somber. "It's for the memorials."

Billy swallowed hard and tried not to let the hurt and pain show. "As long as I don't have to see my mother again. I can't believe she was screaming at the police that *we* were the ones at fault, that we corrupted him. She even went on the fucking news and proclaimed it."

Jordan rubbed Billy's shoulder. "I hate that you don't have anyone to go home to."

Billy gave Jordan an incredulous look and asked, "Why, are you going somewhere? You're the someone I have … to come home to." Billy put his arms around Jordan. "The only someone I want to come home to."

"Awe, that's so sweet." Jordan looked at Billy adoringly. Then he narrowed his eyes at Billy. "What do you want?"

Billy winked and reached around Jordan to squeeze his butt. "That ass."

"Jordan, flirt with the stars on your own time. Get over here!" Lexi yelled, sounding serious, but Jordan saw the coy smile on her face.

Jordan pecked Billy on the lips. "Break a leg," and he took his seat beside Lexi.

"Quiet on set!" Lexi yelled.

The camera assistant moved in front of the set and announced, "Diva Porn Star, Take One." He snapped the clapper board shut, then moved out of the view of the camera.

Lexi reached over and squeezed Jordan's hand. "Action!"

Eric sat in the living room of the bed-and-breakfast he and his lover had run for the past couple years. He was fascinated with the article on his tablet about the man dubbed "The Porn Star Killer" by Jordan Hudson. It was breaking all over the news outlets, and they were even hearing about it up here in the middle of nowhere, Maine.

He looked up when his lover came into the room carrying two steaming cups of coffee. "Hey, Steven. Have you seen the news about this porn star killer?"

Handing his lover one of the cups and sitting down, Steven lied. "I saw something about it. I really didn't pay any attention to it."

Setting the tablet aside, Eric asked, "Aren't you from this area? Did you know any of those guys?"

"No, I was just a shadow back there," he said, closing his eyes as he sipped his coffee. Steven said a silent prayer for the men he left behind when he needed to forge his own path. He remembered the words of the note he left them.

Epilogue

I'm sorry. I have to go. I love you all, but this life isn't for me. Thank you for all you've done for me. Please, don't try to find me. I need to step out of the Shadow.

Love
S
RJL

BOOK CLUB
DISCUSSION QUESTIONS

1) In the beginning, we read about Billy and Teddy. Teddy is in the closet and has a girlfriend but is having intimate relations with Billy. Do you think Teddy really has feelings for Billy or is he just a release?

2) There are several "straight" men in the story that either engage or proposition gay sex from other men. Are these men denying their sexuality or just looking any port in a storm, meaning they are just looking to get off?

3) Jordan doubts himself and his writing at first and doesn't really feel confident until Billy gets involved. Is that something we do—doubt ourselves until someone else believes in us?

4) How do you think Billy views sex?

5) The Country Boyz all went their separate ways and didn't keep in touch. Did they outgrow each other or did they just have different aspirations?

6) Billy's mom tossed him out and wouldn't answer his calls or text, yet she took hismoney. When Billy rushed home to make sure she was okay, she rushed him into the house before the neighbors saw. How do you think she truly felt about Billy?

7) Why do you think Billy doesn't realize that he like Jordan when everyone else can plainly see it?

8) Do you think Keith's parents were upset over that fact he did gay porn or that it was found out?

9) Joe had a lover of another race. They were called names and shunned by the gay community for being an interracial couple. Is this still the case?

10) Cameron isn't in porn,but engaged to Alex who is. Does Cameron have the right to be upset when he finds out about Alex and Dennis? Why or why not?

ROBBY LEWIS IS a gay erotica writer based out of Charleston, South Carolina. When he's not busy with his plants, being a doggy-daddy, or watching the latest Sci-Fi, he can be found creating gay erotica for his readers that challenge conventional sexual roles. He's influenced by such writers as T.J. Klune, Rhys Ford, Jordan Castillo Price, and L.A. Witt. You can keep up with Robby Lewis's latest releases and antics on his social media at <u>Dreams – Robert J. Lewis (robert-j-lewis.com)</u>

More books from
4 Horsemen Publications

LGBT Erotica

LGBT Romance

CRIME, DETECTIVE, AND NOIR

JOE DAVISON
Journey to Hell

MARK ATLEY
Too Late to Say Goodbye
Trouble Weighs a Ton

HORROR, THRILLER, & SUSPENSE

ALAN BERKSHIRE
Jungle

No Place for Happiness
I Hunt You

AMANDA BYRD
Trapped
Moratorium
Medicate

MARIA DEVIVO
Witch of the Black Circle
Witch of the Red Thorn

MARK TARRANT
The Mighty Hook
The Death Riders
Howl of the Windigo
Guts and Garter Belts

ERIKA LANCE
Jimmy
Illusions of Happiness

DISCOVER MORE AT
4HORSEMENPUBLICATIONS.COM